"You're not afraid of me, are you?"

"Why should I be?" Eve countered boldly, ignoring the fact that it had been years since any man had towered over her. "You can't do anything to *me*, after all, and I've got nothing to lose in all of this. You can't really do anything to Ted and Lucie, come to that. You can revoke her trust, or cut her off without a cent, but you can't prevent them from getting married. They intend to do it, anyway—with or without your blessing."

"With or without her money, you mean," Jack objected smoothly. "They could lose that."

"True, but they don't really care, and *I* certainly don't. None of us has anything to lose."

"We shall see."

Elizabeth Barnes lives with her husband and son near Boston, Massachusetts. She likes to see treasures from the past lovingly restored and was instrumental in helping restore the local nineteenth-century church after it was badly damaged by fire. Vintage cars are a long-standing passion of the whole family.

No Love in Return

Elizabeth Barnes

Harlequin Books

TORONTO • NEW YORK • LONDON
AMSTERDAM • PARIS • SYDNEY • HAMBURG
STOCKHOLM • ATHENS • TOKYO • MILAN

Original hardcover edition published in 1987
by Mills & Boon Limited

ISBN 0-373-02972-1

Harlequin Romance first edition April 1989

CHAPTER ONE

EVE'S first thought was that this man couldn't possibly be Jackson Sinclair. In no way did he match her mental image of a middle-aged and bloodless businessman compensating for defects of personality or appearance by attempting to amass as much money as possible. Nothing about this man—this *presence*—suggested the need to compensate for anything! In fact, everything was unexpected, and Eve was briefly exasperated with Lucie for having given such an erroneous picture of her brother. He wasn't even middle-aged, she saw, deciding that Jackson Sinclair gave new meaning to the phrase 'a man in his prime'.

He was tall—very tall, at least six-four, she guessed. At five-ten, she was no slouch herself, but this man towered. He was also exceedingly fit, and not even the impeccably tailored grey pinstripe suit could disguise the broad-shouldered, lean hardness of the man. He didn't look a bit like a bloodless businessman who lived only to make money; he looked like a man who played hard and worked out regularly. There wasn't a spare ounce of flesh on his large frame, and he moved with the natural grace of an athlete.

He was probably in his mid-thirties, although his face seemed younger—deeply tanned skin over an impressive bone structure, with a strong nose and an even stronger chin. His mouth was wide and thin-lipped, which should have suggested asceticism. Instead, it appeared unexpectedly sensual, and a smile of mocking amusement seemed to lurk just beneath the surface. There were only faint lines bracketing his mouth, and none at all on the high forehead. His hair was a sun-streaked dark blond, thick and with considerable body, slanting casually across his brow.

But it was his eyes which impressed Eve most. They were guarded, revealing nothing of himself, but with a careful watchfulness about them which suggested that he missed almost nothing. They were also exceedingly dark against his fair hair, although she couldn't tell if they were a deep blue, grey or even black.

Whatever colour they were, they were formidable eyes, and he was a formidable person, she conceded. There was no use hoping he wasn't Jackson Sinclair; Lucie's reaction had taken care of that. When they had heard the front door close behind him, Lucie had actually jumped and then reached quickly for Ted's hand, clearly seeking reassurance. For a moment the room had been filled with the small sounds of silence—the cheerful crackling of the fire, the steady beat of the long case clock in the corner. Then, beyond the closed door of the room, Eve had heard the low murmur of voices, followed by firm footsteps approaching.

'He's here,' Lucie had said unnecessarily in the brief moment before the door to the library opened and Eve had her first look at him.

Tony had been right, Eve found herself thinking, even as she watched Jackson Sinclair—being very cool about it—take the time to study each of the three faces looking up at him. Damn! she thought. She really ought to have believed what Tony had told her last week! If she had, the reality of this man wouldn't have come as quite such a surprise.

The conversation had come at the end of a long and difficult day, she remembered, thinking back to that evening. By the time the work had been finished, her feet had been sore, her back aching and her face had felt stiff from too much smiling. All day she'd been at the mercy of Tony DeViro's camera lenses and his faintly accented, coaxing voice. 'That's right, darling, give me a little more . . . one of your wicked smiles now . . . and turn, and toss your hair . . . marvellous, darling, couldn't be better!'

But, in the quiet of the little dressing-room, Eve could shed the last of the elegant dresses she had been modelling, wipe her face clean of make-up and slip into her jeans and cotton shirt. She felt human again, she thought with relief as she picked up her coat and her tote bag, preparing to leave the room. She always felt more human when she could strip away the business—the make-up and clothes of a model—and be herself.

'Stay and talk for a while,' Tony suggested as she returned to the now dimly lit studio.

Eve nodded and dropped gratefully into the nearest chair. She'd been talking to Tony for seven years now, she mused, watching as he crossed the room to pour coffee for both of them. She had only been modelling for a year when he had photographed her for the first time, and his perceptive eye had seen what no one else had realised. He

had talked with her for a while after that first
session and then asked bluntly, 'You don't like
modelling, do you?'

'No,' Eve had answered, equally blunt.

'Then why do you do it?' he had demanded, his
accent less pronounced now that the two of them
were alone. 'You're a bright girl—that's obvious.
Surely you could do something else!'

'But I don't know how to do anything that pays
as well,' she had explained, watching the quick
flicker of impatience cross his sharp, clever features.

'Do you care that much for money?'

'Not for myself,' she had begun, and because he
seemed so different from anyone else she had met
in the business—actually interested in her as a
person—she had explained everything.

Her mother had died five years before, when
Eve had been sixteen and her brother Ted only
twelve. Then, just the year before, her father had
also died. 'And there wasn't much insurance,' she
had explained reluctantly, 'just enough to tide us
over until I could begin earning a living. I'd finished
two years of college, taking a liberal arts course,
and I wasn't trained to do anything. My flatmate's
father was in advertising, and he thought I could
have some success as a model. He helped a lot—
put me in touch with several good agencies, and
one of them took me on.

'And I've *got* to earn a lot,' she had confided,
'because my brother is really brilliant. He deserves
a good education, and it wouldn't be fair to let
him down.'

'So you do work you despise to keep your
brother in school,' Tony had summarised with an

understanding smile, and from then on he had taken a personal interest in her. He had used her as his model whenever he could, and he had always been interested in both her life and in her brother's academic progress.

'So,' Tony had begun that evening last week, coming back with their coffee and sitting down across from her, 'how's the budding anthropologist doing? It can't be long until he starts his fieldwork.'

'Less than a year, but I'm not sure he even cares at the moment. He's in love,' Eve explained, unable to repress a smile. 'He's fallen madly in love with an undergraduate who took the Beginning Anthropology course he taught last autumn. Her name is Lucie Sinclair, and she's as much of an orphan as we are—her parents have been dead for some years, and there's just an older brother to pay the bills and make a few of the major decisions.'

'But there's a problem,' Tony observed shrewdly, studying Eve's face.

'Yes.' She sighed as she contemplated this one cloud on Ted and Lucie's horizon. 'Jack—that's Lucie's brother—has decided that Lucie isn't old enough to marry anyone, and that Ted is just after her money. She does have some of her own, I think—perhaps a trust fund,' Eve explained vaguely. 'Ted couldn't care less about that, of course. He doesn't know the first thing about money, and I don't think it's even entered his head that Lucie is financially comfortable. But Jack doesn't realise that, and he's been giving them a terribly hard time about getting married. The latest is that he's threatened to practically disown Lucie—

refuse to even see her if she doesn't break up with Ted.

'But it's gone way beyond that,' she continued, a worried frown marring her forehead. 'They're very much in love, and they're determined to get married before Ted goes off to do his fieldwork. *They* won't give in, and we're all afraid Jack won't either, and the whole thing is tearing Lucie apart. She worships Jack—God knows why. He sounds like a terribly unfeeling person, and . . . ' She trailed off uncertainly as she realised that Tony wasn't really hearing what she was telling him. Instead, he was watching her face with an expression of amusement and something like glee. 'What is it?' she asked.

'You're talking about *the* Lucie Sinclair, aren't you?' demanded Tony with an unholy grin. '*The* Jackson Sinclair's sister!'

'Yes,' Eve agreed rather blankly, wondering why he found that so remarkable. 'That's his name, but why do you call him *the* Jackson Sinclair?'

'Because he is,' Tony explained with considerable relish. 'Good God!' Words failed him for a moment. 'All that money, and I honestly believe you and Ted didn't know it!'

'Is it "all that money"?' Eve asked doubtfully. 'I know there's some involved, but do you mean a *lot*?'

'More than you could ever imagine,' Tony answered airily. 'So much that I'm not sure anyone knows just how much it is.'

'Oh dear,' Eve said softly, shivering at the implication of Tony's words. She'd realised that Lucie was comfortably well off, but Tony made it sound

like wealth of considerably greater magnitude. If
that were the case, then the unknown Jack's objections—which had seemed ridiculously Victorian—
now made perfect sense. 'Are you sure?' she began
again, thinking Tony must be mistaken. 'I'd never
heard of Jackson Sinclair until Ted got to know
Lucie, and surely I would have, if he's as rich as
you say.'

'Not at all,' he answered with depressing
certainty. 'Unless you read the financial columns
on a regular basis, you won't have heard of him.
The man pays a press agent more than you make
in a year to keep his name *out* of the news. He
may even pay more than *I* make in a year,' he
added reflectively, his complacent smile suggesting
that he was, at the moment, contemplating his
undoubtedly huge earnings as a fashion photographer. 'People like Jackson Sinclair live incredibly
discreet lives.'

'Oh dear,' Eve said again, nervously clutching
her mug with both hands. 'What have I gotten
myself into?'

'A fine kettle of fish, I should say,' Tony observed
cheerfully, clearly enjoying the whole idea. 'But
isn't it Ted who's got himself into it?'

'I suppose so,' she agreed absently, her mind
working furiously, 'but I've promised to try to
reason with Jack this weekend, and—— Oh, I can't
even call him Jack now, can I?' she wailed. 'Not if
he's what you say he is.'

'Oh, he is,' Tony assured her, still infuriatingly
cheerful, 'and I don't think he's going to be particularly reasonable. But why are *you* going to try?'

'Because Lucie asked me to,' Eve explained with

a terrible sense of inevitability. 'She said I'd be able to explain the whole thing to him, that he'd listen to me because I'm more his age, and I'm sensible.'

'Did she?' Tony managed before his high, cackling laugh overwhelmed him completely. 'I don't think *he's* going to see it quite that way,' he continued when he had regained his control. 'Where is this grand summit meeting supposed to take place?'

'At his house, somewhere near Boston. Ted and Lucie often spend weekends there, and I'm supposed to fly to Boston Friday afternoon and they'll drive me there. Ted says it's a very nice place,' she added, straying briefly.

'A very nice place,' Tony repeated with wonder in his voice. 'Your brother *does* have his head in the academic clouds, doesn't he? Stonegate isn't just very nice; it's a showplace—priceless antiques, wonderful gardens and an enormous staff.'

'How do you know all this?' demanded Eve. 'If he spends so much money to keep himself out of the news, I don't see how you *can* know so much!'

'I move in the right circles, darling,' Tony answered smugly. 'You'd be amazed at the information I pick up. And I do see him at parties on occasion,' he added casually, 'the sort of parties that never get into the news.'

'Is he as bad as he sounds?' Eve asked quickly, compelled to hear the worst.

'It depends.' He shrugged. 'How bad does it sound to you?'

'Terrible,' Eve admitted bleakly. 'All that money is going to make things so much worse!'

'I should think it would make things considerably better,' Tony put in brightly.

'Not when Jack—Lucie's brother,' Eve corrected quickly, 'thinks Ted's after it.' She sighed heavily. 'If he'd only realise that Ted doesn't know the first thing about money! But I don't suppose he will, and from what Lucie says, he's a terribly rigid man. It sounds as though he lives for his business and nothing else. He's obviously too old and stuffy to believe in anything as random and unpredictable as love.'

'I don't think you've got quite the right picture of him,' cautioned Tony cheerfully. 'I think you're going to be surprised.'

'Why?' asked Eve quickly. 'Is he human after all?'

'I don't know *that*,' he protested, 'but I expect you'll be as much of a surprise to him as he'll be to you. I also think,' he continued, getting up from his chair to indicate that their talk was over, 'that it will take him longer than usual to figure you out. You're such an innocent, darling Eve,' he added obliquely. 'Have fun this weekend,' he called after her as she started to leave the studio, 'and you must tell me all about it as soon as you're back,' he finished with a wicked grin.

Well, she'd certainly have to tell him he'd been right about Jackson Sinclair, Eve acknowledged. She had been watching Lucie's brother and realising just how different he was from other men. He wasn't just larger than life and more attractive than any man had a right to be; he was also the most incredibly self-possessed—and possibly autocratic—person she had ever seen. He was completely at his ease, taking his own sweet time to examine each of them in turn.

Lucie had been first, and his scrutiny had made her nervous and uncertain, completely unlike the girl Eve had known for the last few months. At first, Eve had been surprised that her serious, scholarly brother had fallen in love with someone so relentlessly enthusiastic and self-confident. Then, as she had got to know Lucie better, she had realised why Ted found her so charming. There was something infectious about Lucie's sunny disposition and bubbling personality, but all that was missing now. She was suddenly tentative, watching her brother the way a puppy watches its angry master.

When Jackson Sinclair turned his attention to Ted, Eve was surprised to see that he looked terribly young and just as uncertain as Lucie. The last time she had seen Ted like this had been during the first few months after their father had died and their future had seemed so uncertain. Now, because of Jackson Sinclair's close inspection, she could see the insecure teenager Ted had once been.

But it was her turn to be inspected, she realised. She could tell even before she looked away from Ted and glanced up to meet Jackson Sinclair's cool gaze. She hoped he was seeing what she had tried so hard to achieve—Lucie's reasonable and sensible advocate. Eve had decided to combine those qualities with a suggestion of good taste and quiet elegance. She was wearing an easy wool skirt in shades of maroon and black, with a black blazer, high black leather boots and a soft pink blouse to lessen the effect of the other, darker colours. Her long blonde hair was worn in her usual careful knot on the back of her head, and her only jewellery consisted of small gold hoops in her ears. She had been careful and sparing with her make-up, too, knowing instinctively that she should avoid anything that shrieked 'model'.

Her experience as a model helped her to endure the inspection. She knew how to project an image, how to assume a pose, how to conquer nervousness. But why should she be nervous of him? she asked herself, returning his gaze without flinching. Jackson Sinclair didn't matter to her! For reasons which passed understanding, he mattered to Lucie; she would be very badly hurt if he didn't give his blessing to her marriage to Ted. If that happened, Ted would also feel badly, because he didn't want the two of them to start their marriage under a cloud. But they *would* survive, Eve assured herself with a feeling that was part relief and part malicious pleasure, watching as the man finally completed his inspection of her and then turned back to Lucie.

'I thought we'd agreed that I'd be seeing *you* this weekend,' he said, breaking the long silence he had imposed on all of them. 'You didn't tell me this was going to be a house party.'

'But it's not,' Lucie explained hesitantly, still with the anxious puppy expression on her face. 'I wanted you to meet Ted and Eve, that's all.'

'I see. You might have mentioned it, so that I could explain that this isn't the best time.' He turned away from them long enough to pour himself a drink. It was obvious that he wasn't pleased to have the three of them here, but Eve couldn't decide if he were angry, impatient, or merely tired.

'I've been on the move almost constantly this past week,' he resumed, sipping his drink as he turned back to them. 'If I hadn't agreed to be here this evening—for *you*,' he noted pointedly, 'I'd have spent the night in London and gotten some sleep. You'll pardon me, I hope,' he continued, including Eve and Ted for the first time, 'if I don't linger to make polite conversation.'

'We didn't come for polite conversation,' Lucie ventured, still tentative. 'I wanted you to get to know Ted—and Eve too, of course.'

'Obviously,' he agreed evenly, giving no hint of what he was thinking, 'but surely we'd have started with polite conversation, and that's something I simply can't handle tonight. I'm afraid it will have to wait until morning.' He paused only long enough to drain his glass. 'If you'll excuse me,' he finished abruptly, then left the room.

'Middle-aged indeed!' Eve said aloud when she'd closed her bedroom door behind her. How on earth had Lucie managed to give the impression that her brother was so old? And how much else of what Lucie had told her about him would prove to be just as inaccurate? Lucie was a dear—a sweet girl— but it was obvious that she wasn't the most reliable informant, at least where her brother was concerned!

'He doesn't know *anything* about love,' Lucie had told Eve. 'He was engaged once, years ago, when I was just a child, but she broke it off. He was already cold, and Mummy said this would only make him colder, until he was just like Father. That's why Mummy was so unhappy with Father— because he didn't have an ounce of human feeling. Once Jack was born, he never really bothered with Mummy again. He spent all his time making money, and it's a wonder I ever happened! Of course, I came years later, and I've always thought I must have been nothing but a momentary lapse on Father's part.

'But anyway,' she had continued, reining herself in from her brief digression, 'Jack's just like Father. All he cares about is making money, and he doesn't know the first thing about how it feels to be in love. He has affairs from time to time, but they don't mean anything to him, and he simply can't understand that I'm *in love* with Ted. He thinks Ted is only after my money—which is absurd, of course! Jack makes such a production about money—*making* it matters, although he doesn't seem to care about *spending* it, and he's forever lecturing me about spending too much. That's really the only time he bothers to see me—when he thinks I've spent too much and he wants to give me another lecture!'

But what Eve had seen thus far seemed to contradict what Lucie had told her. If Jackson Sinclair only bothered to see her when he wanted to lecture her, why had he made such an effort to be here this weekend? Nor did this estate fit Lucie's picture of her brother. As Tony had told her, Eve acknowledged, it was a showplace, and the guest-room she had been given was a perfect example of the luxury and comfort of the house.

There were superb antiques—a canopied four-

poster bed, a beautifully carved chest, a fine slant-
topped desk and a graceful dressing-table with
matching mirror above. The curtains at the three
windows, the hangings and spread on the bed were
of a cool green watered silk which matched the
covering of the walls above the white wainscoting.
But for all its elegance, the room was welcoming
and livable in, with a few current magazines on
the table beside the wing-back chair, books on the
table by the bed, and blue and yellow crocuses in
a Chinese export bowl on the dresser. The furniture
was obviously lovingly maintained—dusted and
polished to a high gloss, the brass drawer-pulls
shining.

None of this came cheap, Eve told herself,
instantly uncomfortable at having such mercenary
thoughts. But the point was that Jackson Sinclair
was spending an enormous amount of money on
Stonegate—enough money to ensure that it was
loved, not just maintained. If spending money
hadn't been important to him, he'd have got rid of
the place years ago. To be sure, Lucie had explained
that there had been Sinclairs here for generations,
but a completely cold and calculating Jackson
Sinclair wouldn't have felt bound by tradition. So,
Eve decided, sitting down at the dressing-table,
and automatically beginning to remove the pins
from her hair, she'd better ignore the things Lucie
had told her. It would be far more useful to
remember that the man was *different*—and make
her own decisions about Jackson Sinclair.

Certainly he would do the same. Eve doubted
that the man ever let anyone else's opinions influence him, and she couldn't help wondering what

he thought of her. He probably disapproved, she concluded after a moment's reflection. Given what Tony had told her about hiring a press agent to keep his name out of the news, he must be less than thrilled to think there was a chance of being related—even by marriage—to a model!

Eve contemplated that gloomy thought as she set down her hairbrush and stared back at her reflected image. Her problem was, she thought unhappily, that she looked too much like the model she was. There were the high cheekbones and the classic nose, the generous, almost pouting lips, the slanting eyes which could shade from green to hazel to silvery grey. Even without make-up, there was no disguising the bone structure or the perfect oval of her face. Jackson Sinclair was going to see all that every time he looked at her, and dislike her all the more because she made her living posing for photographers.

Would it help, she wondered, if she told him she wouldn't be a model much longer? At twenty-eight, she was close to being over the hill. Another couple of years and she *would* be, at which time she would have to find a different and less public way to earn a living. She wasn't a Cheryl Tiegs to launch a line of clothing, or a Christie Brinkley to marry a rock star. Unlike many models, she had never considered trying for a career in movies. She had just done her job, posed for the camera, and managed to make enough to keep up with Ted's never-ending tuition payments and expenses—with just enough left over to support herself.

But it wasn't going to last much longer. The camera saw the tiny lines that people didn't notice.

The camera demanded the perfection of dewy freshness, and she was rapidly losing that! Perhaps she could promise Jackson Sinclair that she'd go into some line of work that was very, very private . . .

And perhaps Jackson Sinclair didn't give a damn what she did with her life, she told herself, realising that she was getting silly now. It had been a very long day—three photo sessions and then a mad scramble to make the right shuttle from LaGuardia to Boston, the drive here, the hours listening to Ted and Lucie as they enthusiastically discussed their future, Jackson Sinclair's brief appearance, and now all these pointless thoughts. It was time for bed!

She got up from the dressing-table, turned out the light, then went to open a window. There was the fresh, earthy scent of spring and enough moonlight to cast faint shadows on the terrace and the gardens beyond. Below her and off to the side of the house, she could see two brighter rectangles of light against the terrace—lights burning in the wing to the right of her bedroom. While she still stood by the window, a third and longer rectangle of light materialised, followed by the sound of footsteps and the shadow of a man. Ted going out for a walk, she thought, then realised her mistake as she saw a lighter flare briefly in the darkness.

It was Jackson Sinclair. The flame from the lighter illuminated his profile for an instant as he lit a cigarette, and then there was nothing left except his long black shadow, punctuated by the tiny red glow of the tip of his cigarette. Eve drew back a bit, but she stayed by the window, watching as he crossed the terrace, then stopped to lean against the trunk of the nearest tree.

He stood there for a long time, motionless except for the occasional movement of his cigarette, until she saw it arc as he threw it away. Then his shadow detached itself from that of the tree and he moved on, into the garden. Now he was where the moonlight could reach him, and she could see him more clearly, see that his hands were pushed into his pockets and that his head was bent in concentration.

What was he thinking? she wondered, watching as he slowly paced the formal paths. And why, if he had had such a difficult week, was he still up when the rest of the house was asleep? Because he loved this place, she realised instinctively. She could feel his attachment to this peaceful, settled spot, and she could understand exactly how it affected him. There was such a sense of permanence here; she felt it after only a few hours, and she could understand how much stronger the feeling must be for him, knowing that his family had been here for generations.

That sudden insight told her something unexpected about Jackson Sinclair. He wasn't as completely devoid of emotion as she had thought. He wasn't all cool logic; he did have some feeling after all—an almost passionate attachment to *something*, if not to *anyone*. The thought pleased her, although she couldn't say why, and she was feeling considerably more optimistic as she slipped between sheets which held the fragrance of fresh air and sunshine. They had been hung out to dry, she realised happily as she drifted off to sleep. Her last coherent thought was that while she and Jackson Sinclair might be poles apart on most issues, at least they were in agreement about their feelings for this lovely place.

CHAPTER TWO

Eve awakened to a perfect spring morning, with a hundred different shades of green against the pale blue sky and dew glittering like diamonds where the sunlight caught it on the grass. On a day like this she welcomed the morning run which was an integral part of her daily routine. Usually it was a penance to run the required laps of the perimeter of the little park near her apartment—all grit and litter, the air already laden with exhaust fumes. But running here was going to be a joy, she thought, dressing quickly in her well worn running clothes and tying a scarf around her tangled hair. She crept through the sleeping house, down the stairs and out through the front door. On the top step, under the pillared portico, she debated briefly which way to go. Yesterday, they had come from the left, up the long gravel drive from the gates at the road. But the drive continued to the right, and she chose that way, wanting to see more of the estate.

When she had gained a little distance, she paused to look back at the house, an impressive example of Georgian Colonial architecture. The centre section was a full three storeys tall, with two-storey wings on either side, its regular symmetry relieved only by the elongated Palladian window over the entrance. It commanded the top of a gentle rise, and Eve set off down the drive at a steady pace.

She passed a series of outbuildings, including a small house with white clapboards and black shutters. It must be very old, she decided, noting how the tops of the windows met the fascia board under the low eaves. Early 1700s, she guessed, continuing on until she came to a long, still pond. The drive curved around one side, providing a view back up the hill and a glimpse through the trees of the rooftops and the chimneys of the main house. At the far end of the pond, commanding a slight rise, was—what? she wondered, breaking stride to study the little building. It appeared to be a small Grecian temple, with four graceful white pillars across the front to support the porch, and behind them two small windows flanking the door. A summerhouse of sorts—a folly, she decided, resuming her steady pace.

Ahead, through the trees, she could see a large stable block of the same Georgian design as the house. The drive extended along the length of the building and then turned sharply right. Eve was running harder now; she took the turn at a good clip and abruptly collided with something very solid.

What breath she had left was knocked completely out of her, and there was a moment's disorientation before she realised that someone was gripping her arms and that her head was resting against a firm and unyielding shoulder. She knew, even before she looked up, that she had collided with Jackson Sinclair. She was leaning against a man too tall to be anyone else.

'I *am* sorry,' she said in short bursts, trying to

catch her breath. 'I wasn't paying attention.'

'Are you all right?' he asked, still maintaining his grip on her arms.

'Yes,' she nodded, risking a glance at his face. If the collision had surprised him as much as it had her, it didn't show in his expression. 'I've been running hard, that's all,' she added more evenly, stepping back a pace when he finally released her.

'Obviously,' he agreed, examining her carefully from head to toe, taking in her shabby running outfit, her flushed face and the strands of hair which had escaped from the scarf to cling damply to her forehead. She knew she looked a sight, while he was as impeccably turned out as he had been the night before, although he was in country clothes this morning—tan cords and a dark brown sweater. 'I wouldn't have expected you to be up and about this early,' he told her when he had completed his inspection. If there had been any amusement in his expression, it was gone now—replaced by curiosity.

Eve knew that look; she had seen it plenty of times before, and it answered at least one of her questions about Jackson Sinclair. He knew she was a model; he was looking at her as people did when they knew nothing about the realities of a model's life, when they thought it was all glamour and late nights spent partying. 'I'm always up this early,' she explained, and then decided on impulse to take the war to him, 'but I'm surprised that *you* are.'

'Are you?' he asked, leaning back against the corner of the stable, hands in his pockets, making it clear that he was in no hurry to be rid of her. 'Why?'

'Because you were up so late.' She stopped.

Having watched him from her window last night suddenly seemed an invasion of his privacy, something she'd rather he did not know she had done. 'What with the time change,' she continued, trying to cover her slip, 'you must have been tired. You came from London, didn't you? That would make it five hours later for you than for us.'

'Of course,' he agreed mildly enough, but she could tell from the sudden spark in his eyes that he knew she had watched him, 'but I recover quickly.'

'I would too,' she said impulsively, 'if I always came back here. I'd always want to be up early, if I lived here!'

'Then why do you always get up early, if you'd rather not?' he asked, as though the contradiction actually interested him.

'Because I have to,' she explained. 'I have to run every day—I can't afford not to. I like to eat—and food is something a model ought to avoid at all costs—so I do an hour's penance every morning, running off my indiscretions.'

'And that's all it takes?' he enquired sceptically, his expression suggesting that he assumed she was guilty of countless other indiscretions.

'I live a very sheltered life,' she snapped, instantly on the defensive. 'You shouldn't believe everything you hear about models, Mr Sinclair.'

'Jack,' he corrected, shifting moods again, favouring her with a disarming smile, 'and I'll try to keep an open mind, Miss Foster—or is it *Ms* Foster?'

'Eve,' she corrected in her turn, but it was little more than an automatic response. Her mind was elsewhere, grappling with the idea of calling this giant of a man Jack. She wasn't convinced she *could* call him Jack; she'd probably end up calling him nothing at all.

'You might as well say it,' he prompted, making it clear that she'd been silent too long.

'Say what?'

'Whatever it is you're thinking so busily.'

'I'm wondering if you really will try to keep an open mind,' she explained, deciding she couldn't go into the business of using his first name. Besides, there was no time like the present to get to the heart of the matter. 'Will you try to keep an open mind about Ted and Lucie?'

'I wondered when we'd get to that,' he observed pleasantly. 'That's why you came, isn't it?—not so that I could meet both Ted and what family he has, but so that you could plead his case.'

'Plead *their* case,' she corrected, seeing no point in denying it.

'If you like,' he agreed coolly, 'but this is neither the time nor the place. Come to my office at ten, and don't bring the young lovers with you. I prefer that we discuss it between ourselves at this point.'

'If you like,' she answered, daring to copy both his words and his tone, 'but strictly speaking, they're not lovers, you know.'

'I didn't.' Jack detached himself from the stable wall, extending to his full height again. 'You're not afraid of me, are you?'

'Why should I be?' she countered boldly, ignoring the fact that it had been years since any man had towered over her. 'You can't do anything to me, after all, and I've got nothing to lose in all this.

You can't really do anything to Ted and Lucie, come to that. You can revoke her trust, or cut her off without a cent, but you can't prevent them from getting married. They intend to do it anyway—with or without your blessing.'

'With or without her money, you mean,' he objected smoothly. 'They could lose that.'

'True, but they don't really care, and *I* certainly don't. None of us has anything to lose.'

'We shall see.' He smiled just as pleasantly as before, then turned and started up the drive towards the house.

'He wants to see me at ten,' Eve reported to Ted and Lucie over breakfast. *He* wasn't with them. Perhaps he had eaten while she had been finishing her run or showering and getting dressed after she had returned to the house. This time she was wearing well tailored slacks and a casual jersey top—some of her country clothes, she had reflected with a smile when she had finished dressing. Of course, all her effort had probably been for nothing; Jack had caught her in her shabby running outfit, and that had pretty well ruined any impression she had been trying to make. 'We're going to talk about the two of you.'

'How did you manage that?' demanded Lucie, leaning eagerly across the table.

'We met when I was out running, and I didn't have to manage anything. He suggested it,' Eve told her, giving an edited version of their meeting.

'Oh.' Lucie briefly digested that. 'I wonder why.'

'Because he knows that's why you brought me along,' Eve explained patiently. 'To plead your

case, as he put it. He doesn't miss very much—
surely you know that!'

'Yes. He really doesn't miss *anything*,' Lucie
admitted with a guilty smile. 'It's just that I always
hope he *will*. What did you think of him this
morning?' she continued quickly. 'Was he as rude
as he was last night?'

'But he wasn't rude last night,' Eve objected
mildly. 'Just tired. And he was reasonably pleasant
this morning. Forbearing, anyway,' she reflected,
'although I'm not sure why. He couldn't have
gotten that much sleep.'

'He never sleeps very much,' Lucie explained
easily. 'He's always too busy making money.'

There it was again, Eve told herself, hiding a
smile as she sipped her coffee—Lucie's view of
him, which varied greatly from her own. Having
met Jack, having seen a little more of him and
been exposed to flashes of undeniable charm, she
no longer believed he spent all his time making
money. She was willing to bet that he had his
moments, and plenty of attractive women willing
to fill them.

His office was in the south wing, reached by a
narrow cross corridor off the central hall, in the
wing where Eve had seen the lights last night,
where he had been before he went out to walk in
the garden. The wing was very different from the
rest of the house, she realised instantly. The
proportions were smaller in scale, the ceiling lower,
and the floor of simple wide boards, rather than
the elegant parquet behind her.

First came a kind of ante-room with a fanlight

door to her left, clearly leading to the terrace. Straight ahead was a second door, this one open. Hesitating on the threshold, she saw that the room beyond was more of a study than an office. The few antiques managed to harmonise surprisingly well with the severely simple lines of the modern desk in front of the two east windows, and the room felt even more homey and lived in than the other rooms in the house.

'This is what's left of an older house, isn't it?' she asked, addressing Jackson Sinclair for the first time. He was seated behind the desk, his back to the windows, and she knew he had been watching her while she examined the room. 'Lucie says there have been Sinclairs here for generations, but it was obvious that the rest of the house is too new for that. It can't be more than a hundred years old, I should think.'

'Close,' he agreed, leaning back in his chair. 'Built in 1875, in fact.'

'And this part,' she continued, forgetting for the moment why she was here. 'About a hundred years earlier?'

'Close again. About 1790—just after the Revolution. The family has actually been here nearly three hundred years. When you were running, you may have noticed the little house just down the drive from here. That's the original family home— 1695.'

'Yes, I thought so,' Eve agreed with satisfaction, and caught his sharp look of enquiry.

'You're a student of architecture?' he asked, recovering quickly.

'Not really. It's just that I read a lot, and I like

old houses. You can't help but pick up a fair bit of information,' she explained, pleased to have caught him by surprise. 'Your family seems to take quantum leaps forward, every hundred years or so,' she observed, taking one last look around before she sat down across the desk from him. 'It's your turn, isn't it?' she asked, amused by the thought.

'I haven't got a son,' he said evenly.

'But you might yet. You certainly *could*,' she pointed out, then remembered the girl who had skipped out at the last minute—leaving him practically at the altar, Lucie had said. 'But that's really none of my business, is it?' she finished quickly, hoping she hadn't put her foot in it.

'No, but perhaps *you* think it is,' he said, a hard edge to his voice making his displeasure clear. 'Are you thinking that—if I don't have a son—your brother's son can take the next quantum leap?'

'No. Why should I be?' she asked directly. 'Ted isn't even married yet; I'd hardly be planning his family.'

'But Lucie is *my* only family, my only heir. If your brother marries her, he could find himself married to an extremely wealthy woman—so wealthy as to make her current income look like very small change.'

Well, he hadn't wasted much time, Eve acknowledged, feeling an irrational sense of disappointment. She liked him better when he wasn't being cold and suspicious. 'You really think Ted is after the money, don't you?' she said.

'Yes, and I'd prefer that he didn't get it.'

'Then cut Lucie out of your will, for heaven's

sake!' Bother the man! she thought sourly, staring
across the desk at him. She'd been pleased to think
that Lucie was wrong about him, pleased to think
she could see him more clearly. Now he was
spoiling all that, and her disappointment gave her
words a harder edge, encouraged her to be a little
more sarcastic than wise. 'Cut her out of your will,
or get married and have scads of children of your
own!' She didn't care now that he'd had an
unhappy romance, or that she might be striking a
nerve. 'That ought to solve the problem!'

'I prefer not to take such drastic measures,' Jack
said drily, 'but I don't trust your brother.'

'That's absurd,' snapped Eve, then forced herself
to make an attempt to be reasonable. 'Look, I
realise you don't know Ted, but I can assure you
that money simply doesn't matter to him. His only
concern is that there shouldn't be a breach between
you and Lucie, and it bothers him that you seem
to be so fixated on the issue of money. Frankly, it
bothers me too.'

'I'm sure it does,' he agreed coolly. 'The two of
you must hate the thought that I can prevent you
from getting your hands on it.'

'That's even more absurd,' she told him,
impatient again. 'You make us sound like a couple
of fortune-hunters, and we're not!'

'That's difficult for me to believe. Your brother
has never made any reasonable attempt to support
himself,' he continued, as though ticking items off
a list. 'Nor has he made anything more than token
payment for his education. And you've found a
suitably sybaritic means of earning a marginal
living at best.'

'If you think there's anything luxurious—even easy—about being a model, you're mad!' she exclaimed. 'It was the only thing I could *do* when Daddy died, and it's hellish hard work. And it's hardly a marginal living,' she continued quickly. There was no point in dwelling on how hard she worked. 'It may seem marginal to you, but I can assure you that I make a very good living, quite enough to support Ted and myself, and to pay for his education.'

'Only barely,' Jack contradicted, completely unmoved, 'and it hasn't always been quite enough, has it? There are those two outstanding loans.'

'Which I'm paying off,' Eve retorted, then paused as his words actually registered. 'You've had us investigated, haven't you? What was it? A kind of glorified credit check?'

'Something like that,' he agreed evenly. 'I wanted to know just what sort of people had latched on to my sister. It's all here, if you're interested,' he offered, sliding a manila file across to her side of the desk. 'You may read it, if you like.'

'No.' Instinctively, she drew back in her chair, wanting to put as much distance as possible between herself and the offending file. 'What an unpleasant world you live in, Mr Sinclair—to always be thinking the worst of people, to pay to have them investigated so that you can confirm your poor judgment!'

'Neither I nor the world I live in are the issue here,' he told her, and for the first time she heard irritation in his voice. 'They don't belong in this discussion.'

'But they do,' she told him, momentarily

diverted, almost amused, 'although I wouldn't have called this a discussion. We're having an argument, Mr Sinclair—in case you hadn't noticed. And you're as much a part of it as I am. It's your attitude that's making things so difficult for Ted and Lucie——'

'And for you,' he interrupted smoothly, the cool veneer concealing his anger. 'Life would be much more pleasant for you if your brother married money, although I'm surprised you haven't done it yourself. I understand many models do.'

'Only because most rich men are fools, and some foolish enough to want to marry models,' Eve countered just as evenly. She knew she was being neither wise nor prudent, but the temptation to tell this man exactly what she thought of him was too great to resist. 'Besides, like you, I prefer not to take such drastic measures.'

'You'll leave it to your brother, in fact,' he suggested sarcastically. 'See that he does the job for you.'

'If you're trying to say I did anything to arrange this romance between Ted and Lucie, you're wrong. I didn't even know Lucie existed until four months ago, when she and Ted came to New York for Christmas, and they were already very much in love, so don't accuse me of trying to arrange for my brother to marry money!'

'But you're not averse to taking the main chance when it presents itself, are you? I expect you immediately saw the possibilities *I* present!'

'Your conceit is showing, Mr Sinclair,' she said sweetly. 'Or your paranoia.'

'Conceit, perhaps,' he conceded without

expression, 'but it's hardly paranoia. I know that large sums of money attract the worst kinds of people, but Lucie hasn't learned that yet. She's too young to have developed the necessary caution, and certainly too young to be thinking of marriage.'

'But she's really not, you know,' Eve tried again. 'I realise she's only twenty, but she's very mature in a lot of ways, and she very much wants some stability in her life. I don't mean to insult you— any more than I already have,' she added, 'but it's obvious from what she says that you haven't had a great deal of time for her; she's spent far more time with servants. Now she and Ted both want stability and permanence. They have so much in common—don't you see? That's why they want to belong to each other!'

'And I'm supposed to believe that your brother can give Lucie this stability she craves?' Jack asked sarcastically, but Eve suspected she'd struck a nerve. 'Perhaps Lucie believes he will, but it's obvious that he's only interested in the financial aspects.'

'That's not true,' Eve cut in quickly. 'I don't think Ted even knows what financial aspects *are*, for heaven's sake! He's hopeless when it comes to money—he doesn't think about it, he doesn't talk about it. If you tried to have this kind of argument with him, he'd wonder what on earth you were talking about. He'd think you were either mad or a member of some newly discovered tribe with strange cultural patterns.

'I feel sorry for you, Mr Sinclair,' she told him, and had the satisfaction of seeing a brief flicker of expression in his eyes. 'My brother is going to

marry your sister, whether you like it or not. The
only difference for us will be that *I'll* support them
until Ted has his doctorate and starts teaching.
But you'll have nothing—no family left at all.
You're a hard man, and you know nothing about
love—which is why you're so alone! And you'll be
even more alone when you lose Lucie,' she finished
with a flourish as she got up and left the room.

For an hour Eve walked—down the drive towards
the stables, around the perimeter of the pond,
across the wide field beyond and then into the
woods that enclosed it. When she finally felt she
had achieved a measure of calm, she started back
to the house, meeting Ted and Lucie on the drive.

'Well?' demanded Lucie expectantly. 'How did
it go?'

'Not very well, I'm afraid,' Eve admitted,
concentrating on the gravel beneath her feet so
that she wouldn't have to meet their eyes. 'I suppose
you could say we argued,' she added cautiously.

'Oh, well!' Lucie dismissed that as of no impor-
tance. 'Jack argues with everyone! He's always so
determined to have his own way that arguments
are inevitable. Of course the two of you argued!
I'd have been surprised if you hadn't.

'But the thing is,' she continued happily, and
Eve lacked the courage to stop her, 'that he actually
does listen. You think his mind is so closed that
he hasn't heard a word you've said, but a surprising
amount does get through. Then later you find out
that he's changed his mind, that he's prepared to
be reasonable after all. I know you had good
arguments for him, and that's what counts. Believe

me,' she finished, 'it will all work out. We'll see him at dinner, and perhaps he'll have already thought it over and have something nice to say.'

There was no chance of that, Eve thought grimly as she prepared to go down to dinner. She felt as though she was dressing for her own execution, taking particular pains with her hair and her make-up—as though how she looked might provide some defence against the disaster awaiting them all.

'Nothing will help,' she said aloud to her reflected image when she was finally ready. She had her hair up in the same loose knot, both her pink wool dress and the judicious use of blusher helping to hide the paleness which was the result of nerves. Or fear, she amended silently as she went down the broad staircase and followed the sound of voices to the library.

Nothing about the evening went as Eve had expected. It was all very pleasant and civilised, if a bit superficial—played out like a dramatic presentation of the good and gracious life. The scene was perfect—muted colours and tasteful décor, fine antiques, fresh flowers, good food and wine, a fire burning on the hearth and soft music as a background for conversation.

Ted, Lucie and Jack Sinclair were talking pleasantly enough when Eve appeared at the door to the library. 'Here she is,' observed Ted, spotting her first. 'You're late, old girl.'

'Not too late,' Jack Sinclair said easily, nothing at all like the cold-eyed enemy she had faced across his desk that morning. 'There's still time for a drink. What can I get you, Eve?'

'Sherry,' she answered automatically, trying to work out why things seemed so pleasant.

'I thought you might have fallen asleep,' Lucie explained from her spot beside Ted. 'You must be exhausted after all the running and walking you've done today.'

'Perhaps she's just bored,' Jack suggested, but without any malice, coming across the room to hand Eve her glass. 'This place offers very little excitement to someone accustomed to city life.' As Eve took the glass, their fingers touched briefly. His were warm against the icy coldness of hers, she noted absently, wondering if he was as aware of the contrast as she. 'Were you bored, Eve?' he asked with a disarming smile.

'No,' she answered shortly, incapable of anything more.

'Eve likes the country best,' explained Ted, exhibiting more in the way of social graces than Eve had ever seen before. 'We grew up in the country, and she never wanted to leave. I remember when she'd have to go back to school after vacations, how she'd walk for hours on her last day home—saying goodbye to everything, she told me once.'

'I'm adaptable,' Eve said briefly, wishing they would stop talking about her, that she would stop being the focus of attention, that Jack Sinclair would stop watching her so closely.

Perhaps the others sensed her discomfort, because the conversation did turn away from her, into more general channels. Lucie seemed as bubbly and enthusiastic as ever, although Eve noted that she was careful never to bring up the subject of marriage. She must know, Eve decided. Even though nothing was being said, Lucie had to sense her brother's feelings, but she was managing to keep well hidden any concern or unhappiness she might be feeling. Nor did Ted appear in the least concerned; in fact, he carried a great deal of the conversation. Eve was still too confused—too dazed!—to do more than offer an occasional word or two.

Her only really awkward moment came during dinner, on one of the few occasions when she did attempt to contribute to the conversation. They were discussing the estate, and Ted expressed casual interest in the little house over the brow of the hill. 'It looks old,' he commented, 'or is it just a reproduction?'

'Very old,' Eve supplied, momentarily forgetting her preoccupation. 'Built in 1695. I know because——' She stopped abruptly, wondering what she ought to call the enigma seated to her left.

'Jack,' he prompted easily, perceiving her dilemma.

'—because Jack told me,' she finished uncomfortably, risking a quick glance in his direction.

He was actually enjoying this, she realised, feeling even more confused as she looked away again. There had been a wicked gleam in his eyes, and a smile of mocking amusement was very much in evidence. But only when he looked directly at her, she discovered as the evening continued. She lost count of the number of times she felt his eyes on her and looked up to see that expression. Each time, she watched it disappear when he looked at either Lucie or Ted. He *knew*, she told herself. He knew exactly what she was thinking, that she was dying of curiosity, wondering why he was permitting things to proceed so pleasantly, why he hadn't already stated his objections and burst Ted and Lucie's balloon.

And she would have asked him why, she decided, if only she had had the chance. But he took great pains to see that the opportunity didn't present itself. Even when Lucie decided that she wanted to walk in the garden with Ted, Eve was denied a moment alone with Jack, was forced to watch silently as he rose from his chair.

'And if Eve doesn't mind being left to her own devices, I'll try to get a little more work done,' he explained politely. 'This visit is pleasant enough, but it's raising hell with my schedule,' he added without rancour.

He played the same game the next morning and into the afternoon, making sure that the only times Eve saw him were when the others were present. She supposed it didn't matter, that she really didn't need to know why he was being so pleasant to Ted and Lucie. She told herself that it was probably better not to ask.

There was nothing to be gained by knowing his reasons, and a great deal could be lost if she provoked another row. Perhaps Jack would change his opinion of Ted, Eve decided hopefully, determined to do nothing to prevent that admittedly slim possibility. By mid-afternoon, she had managed to convince herself that it was just as well that he'd prevented another confrontation, and it came as a definite shock when she discovered that he had apparently changed his mind.

CHAPTER THREE

IT STARTED in the late afternoon, when Ted decided that the three of them ought to leave before the weekend traffic got any worse. 'We'll drop you at the airport, of course,' he told Eve, but Jack had other plans.

'There's no need for that,' he objected smoothly. 'It would be easier for her to go back with me tomorrow morning.'

'But I can't,' Eve objected. 'I've got a booking at ten, so I couldn't possibly leave in the morning.'

'I plan to leave here by four,' Jack explained as smoothly as before, but there was determination behind his words, and Eve had the terrible feeling that he was going to get his way. 'You can be at your apartment by seven, which ought to give you time enough. It will be easier for Ted and Lucie too. They won't have to go out of their way to drop you at the airport, and you won't have to fight crowds. It's the only logical thing to do.'

As far as he was concerned, the discussion was closed, and Eve's problem was that she couldn't think of any acceptable objection. There was nothing to do but accept the inevitable and hope the evening wouldn't be completely unendurable.

Later, when she looked back on that evening, Eve wasn't sure what to make of it, but she did know that 'unendurable' was not the correct description. For most of the evening, Jack deliberately steered the conversation into safe and easy channels— books and music and such practical details as what time she would need to get up the next morning. She was learning that he had an uncanny knack for orchestrating things to suit his purpose.

Polite conversation continued until they had finished dinner and returned to the library for coffee, and then Eve finally had her chance.

'Why?' she asked quickly, once the maid had brought the tray and then left them alone. She had had enough of being put off, and she didn't intend it to continue. 'Why did you want me to stay on after Ted and Lucie left?'

'Because you're dying of curiosity,' Jack explained easily, indicating that she should pour for them both. 'I take it black,' he added unnecessarily; she had already noticed that. 'And being alone gives you the chance to ask the question that's been burning you up since last night.'

'I've decided not to,' she said shortly. There was no sense pretending she didn't know what he was talking about. 'Besides, if that's all you had in mind, there were plenty of opportunities for us to be alone.'

'True, but not such a good one as this.' While she poured their coffee, he had been busy at the drinks cabinet, and now he returned with brandy for both of them. 'To be perfectly honest, I find young love cloying,' he continued as he sat down at the far end of the couch, stretching his long legs out to the fire. 'I saw no reason why the two of us had to be saddled with such a touching display.

We're two adults, after all.'

'I don't see what that's got to do with anything,' Eve objected warily. Their isolation in this part of the house, coupled with dim light, soft music and the warmth of the fire, was creating an uncomfortable sense of intimacy. 'That's irrelevant, Mr Sinclair,' she said more firmly.

'Jack,' he corrected automatically, 'and perhaps you're right.' He paused to sip his brandy, then resumed with a disarming smile, 'You're wondering why I didn't get all heavy-handed and Victorian in restating my objections to the marriage. That's what you expected, isn't it?'

'Yes,' she agreed briefly.

'But I rarely do what people expect,' he explained almost apologetically, pausing long enough to light a cigarette. 'In this case, I've decided to let things run their course, to let Lucie assume that there's a chance of getting my approval. She's an incurable optimist, so she's very pleased with life—and me— at the moment.'

'That's cruel!'

'No, only rational,' he corrected mildly. 'Forbidden fruit tastes sweetest, and the last thing I want right now is for Lucie to think of your brother as forbidden fruit. If there's none of the high drama of star-crossed lovers, I think she'll tire of Ted very quickly.'

'I think you're wrong,' Eve said carefully. 'In fact, I know you are.'

'Well, time will tell, won't it?' he enquired pleasantly. 'Lucie says they must be married by the time your brother starts his fieldwork, and he told me he won't be leaving for nearly a year. There's no great rush,' he finished reflectively.

'You're mad,' Eve said faintly, eyeing him with a kind of morbid wonder. 'You think you can manipulate your sister's life and her emotions the same way you manage a business deal. But you *can't*! They'll still get married, but Lucie will hate you for what you've done. I'm not sure she'll ever forgive you!'

'Doesn't that please you?' he asked, managing to sound both amused and slightly surprised. '*You* take such a dim view of me that I should think you'd want Lucie to hate my guts.'

'No, not that,' Eve denied quickly. 'Family is important—at least it ought to be. I don't want Lucie to think she's lost her only blood relative. That wouldn't be fair.'

'Not fair to Lucie, or to me as well?'

'I don't know.' She stared across at him, wishing she could read his expression. 'I'm not sure if any of this matters to you—if *she* really matters.'

'Oh, she matters, all right,' Jack said softly, staring down at his glass. 'Do you really think I'd permit myself to be quite so distracted by all this if she didn't?

'And perhaps you're right after all,' he continued, looking up again, his eyes holding hers. 'Perhaps you and your brother aren't after the money; perhaps he and my sister really do have the kind of love that endures—if there is such a thing.'

'Well,' said Eve slowly, human enough to feel a small sense of triumph, 'that's quite an admission, coming from you.'

'Isn't it?' he asked with a twisted smile. 'Perhaps I'd better think of this year as something more than a clever game of cat and mouse. If my initial impression is right, I've lost nothing. Otherwise——

He hesitated briefly. 'You did say that instead of using private detectives, I should have been getting to know Ted. This year will certainly accomplish that, and I just might discover I'm wrong.'

'There's no "might" about it,' Eve corrected firmly. 'You *are* wrong, and you'll realise it, unless you're more of a fool——'

'Than you already think I am,' he supplied helpfully when she stopped dead.

'I shouldn't have said that,' she offered apologetically.

'Why not?' he asked with a disarming smile. 'Just because you've wrung a concession from me it doesn't mean you've got to start being tactful. I like you better when you're being blunt and outspoken.'

'That's an interesting line,' she observed carefully, thinking she ought to do something to break his new mood. 'I can't think why you bother.'

'To please you, I suppose—and that's not a line. You struck a surprising number of nerves yesterday morning, said a number of things I'd have preferred not to hear.'

'And because of that, you want to please me?' she asked sceptically.

'I know. In fact, very little about this weekend makes much sense,' he continued, consulting his watch. 'It's nearly ten, which doesn't leave much time for sleeping, if we're to leave here at four. I assume that models *are* supposed to try to get their beauty sleep,' he teased as he stood up.

'When they can,' agreed Eve, relieved that he

had finally broken the strange mood between them. 'Could someone wake me about half an hour before you want to leave?' she asked, getting to her feet so that she wouldn't have to crane her neck to see his face.

'No problem,' he assured her, then walked silently beside her as they left the library and crossed the centre hall.

At the foot of the stairs she turned to face him, feeling she ought to acknowledge the softening of his position. 'Thank you,' she began awkwardly, 'for at least being willing to give Ted a chance.'

'Am I forgiven?' asked Jack, smiling down at her.

'I don't know.' She shook her head, confused and suddenly shy. The hallway was dark except for a dim lamp at the top of the stairs and the even dimmer light from the library. The two of them were very close, standing in the shadows, and the mood of intimacy was upon them again. 'I'm not sure there's anything to forgive,' she added uneasily, but he didn't appear to have heard. He was watching her with a strange intensity, and she knew what was going to happen even before he drew her into his arms.

When he kissed her, she could feel the tension between them—a powerful current that left her shaken. She had been kissed before, but never like this, she realised, feeling dazed, her hands instinctively gripping his shoulders. This was something very different—all promise and wild excitement and need—his need and hers so perfectly joined that it was impossible to separate the two, and almost as difficult to step back a pace and grip the banister when he finally released her.

'You didn't even try to make that happen,' he observed after a moment, staring down at her. 'Remarkable. Goodnight, Eve.'

She turned to go slowly up the stairs, knowing that he watched her until she reached the turning and disappeared from view.

Perhaps she'd only dreamed that kiss, Eve told herself the next morning as she settled into her corner of the rear seat of a long, dark grey Mercedes limousine. Certainly Jack gave no sign that he remembered the moment at the foot of the stairs when passion had briefly flared between them.

'Sorry, but I'm afraid this is going to be a working trip for me,' he began as soon as they were under way. 'Will it bother you if I do some dictating?'

'Of course not,' Eve assured him, reflecting that he didn't sound sorry at all. He sounded cool and impersonal, too busy to spare her more than a brief glance before he began to work.

There was a decided distance about him today, one she found disconcerting and even intimidating. It was difficult to believe that this was the man with whom she had argued so fiercely or the man she had found herself liking just after they had collided at the stable that first morning. It was even more difficult to believe that this was the same man who had asked if he had been forgiven— just before he had kissed her.

She kept returning to that kiss, she realised uneasily—dwelling on it because it had had such a profound effect on her. Jack was probably a master, she conceded with a private smile, but he hadn't forced himself on her, and she hadn't simply endured his kiss. She had *responded*—something she honestly couldn't remember ever doing before. She found that thought vaguely depressing—to have reached the advanced age of twenty-eight without ever before having responded to a man's kiss. Even more depressing was the knowledge that she had responded to *this* man, who was so far removed from her in every way.

Even though he was sitting only a couple of feet from her, he was completely unaware of her presence. He had been dictating for some time now, and random snatches of what he was saying kept slipping into her thoughts: ' . . . cost overrun factors must be studied . . . accounting must be involved to a greater extent . . . proposal unacceptable as it stands . . . '

Jackson Sinclair was unacceptable too, she mused, or at least her response to him had been. She had to remember that she didn't mean anything to him and never would. To imagine more was pointless, an invitation to disappointment . . .

'Time to wake up.'

'Oh!' She opened her eyes, blinking at the light. 'I didn't mean to go to sleep . . . I'm sorry.'

'I don't know why,' Jack told her, smiling. 'I've been working the whole time. Time to change to the plane,' he explained, getting out of the car and turning back to offer his hand. 'It's right over there.'

It was a private jet, and quite unlike any plane Eve had ever flown on. The interior was all leather, deep pile carpeting and burl walnut, reminding her of a small and very narrow room. Three easy chairs faced a fourth across a well equipped desk. Jack sat there, of course, returning to his work just as soon as they had taken off and the steward had served coffee.

Eve took the paperback she was currently reading from her bag and opened it, but she didn't start reading immediately. Instead, she found herself wondering if there was any special woman in Jack's life, someone who occasionally travelled with him and managed to attract his attention in a way that *she* certainly didn't. Perhaps, she decided, although she didn't think Jack would allow himself to be involved with any woman on a grand scale. In spite of momentary lapses like last evening's, he wasn't completely human, she reminded herself as a warning, then turned her attention to her book.

'What are you reading?'

'Something on paleoanthropology that Ted passed on to me,' she explained, realising that the plane was starting its descent. 'I *like* paleoanthropology,' she added firmly as she saw his sceptical expression.

'You'd better not let many people know that,' he cautioned. 'You'll get a reputation as a blue-stocking.'

'Most of the people I work with notice what I'm reading and think I'm a bit odd,' she agreed. 'Modelling isn't the most interesting job in the world, you see,' she continued. 'There's a lot of waiting around while they rearrange the lights and decide they're ready for you. I always have a book with me, and I'm never bored.'

'Then I shouldn't have worried, should I?' he asked with a disarming smile. 'Even if you'd been wide awake for the whole trip, you wouldn't have felt neglected.'

'I don't believe you *did* worry,' she told him, and this time he grinned.

'True. I quit worrying years ago. I came to the conclusion that it makes more sense to do something to correct a situation than to worry about it.'

'But you can't always correct a situation,' Eve suggested doubtfully. 'There must be at least a few that you can't do anything about.'

'Not many,' he answered coolly, whatever about him that had been human fast slipping away, 'and I've learned that the situations where I can't do anything really aren't important—not worth the effort. I simply ignore them and walk away.'

'I see,' said Eve automatically, unaccountably depressed that he had made his extraordinary detachment quite so clear.

Eve was already hard at work, cleaning up a weekend's accumulation of clutter—the remains of several meals, an untidy heap of Sunday papers, various items of discarded clothing—when her flatmate arrived home that evening.

'Sorry,' Jane said so unrepentantly that Eve couldn't prevent a smile. 'I guess I did let things get a bit out of hand.'

'You always do, when I'm not around,' Eve pointed out calmly. She and Jane had been sharing the apartment for nearly three years, and they complemented each other very well. It was Jane who had selected the bright lengths of fabric to cover the shabby couch and easy chairs, and who frequently brought home sprightly little touches—cheap prints, wicker baskets, bizarre bits of pottery—which added life to the place. In exchange, Eve was quite happy to handle the routine tasks of housekeeping, finding them familiar and comforting after her artificial days posing for the camera.

'Well,' Jane prompted now with dramatic emphasis, 'you might tell me how the weekend went!' A thin, intense redhead, Jane was, for all her worldly sophistication, a romantic at heart. 'You might have told me what Ted's gotten himself involved in,' she finished reproachfully.

'I didn't know either,' Eve explained. 'It isn't as though I've been keeping any secrets. How did *you* find out?' she added as the thought occurred to her.

'Tony called last night, dying to know how the weekend went. He does love to gossip, doesn't he?' Jane demanded, momentarily diverted. 'But he's fun.'

'And he told you all about this—this mess,' said Eve, resigning herself to more in the way of explanation than she might have liked.

'Since you weren't here to tell him what happened, he told me all about Jack Sinclair. The whole thing's absolutely fascinating, and there's no telling where it may end!'

'What do you mean?' asked Eve, not liking Jane's expectant look. 'Jack's either going to give Ted and Lucie his blessing, or he's not. Those are the only two possible endings,' she finished firmly, but Jane had already stopped listening.

'Jack,' she repeated, pouncing on the name. 'You call him *Jack*?'

'Why not? We can hardly go on being formal when his sister is going to marry my brother! We're going to be family—more or less.'

'Well, I hope it's less,' pronounced Jane vaguely, 'or possibly more. I'm not sure which I mean, but it seems a heavensent opportunity.'

'What does?'

'Lucie's brother, of course.' Jane looked across at Eve with a pitying expression. 'Hasn't it occurred to you yet? Tony says he's not yet forty and considerably better looking than your average Croesus, and he's single . . . Perhaps the two of you will fall in love.'

'There's no chance of that,' Eve retorted sharply, and proceeded with a recital of Jack Sinclair's less than desirable attributes, until she was sure Jane no longer entertained any thoughts of him as a potential love interest.

That exercise took nearly an hour, and Eve had no sooner finished than Tony arrived on her doorstep for the totally unprecedented purpose of taking Eve out to dinner. 'Nothing pretentious,' he assured her. 'We'll be very casual, so you needn't change. I expect the food will be dreadful, but I simply must hear how the weekend went.'

The food was anything but dreadful—trust Tony! Eve thought with affection—and he did manage to hear nearly all of how the weekend had gone. Unlike Jane, Tony appeared sincerely interested in Ted and Lucie. He listened patiently as Eve laid out all Jack's objections, their argument, and most of his behaviour during the weekend. She chose not to mention Jack's few flattering remarks, or the kiss which had ended the previous evening.

'And what did you think of him?' Tony asked her when her long recital had finally ended.

'Well,' she began slowly, carefully, 'it's just as you said—he's different. I felt as though I could never be sure about him. Just when I'd think I knew what kind of man he was, he'd change—stop being what I thought he was, and become something completely different. I think he's basically a hard man, though, and very remote, but he *was* confusing.'

'May I give you some advice?' Tony asked gravely, his eyes holding hers.

'Of course.'

'Make sure he gives you what *you* want. Don't settle for what he's prepared to give; don't settle for crumbs when there's a chance you might be able to have the whole cake.'

'But I don't want anything from him,' Eve protested uneasily, 'and he certainly doesn't intend to give me anything. That's nonsense!'

'Perhaps,' Tony agreed with an obscure smile. 'Time will tell, won't it?'

If Tony and Jane were expecting to see evidence of a blossoming romance between Eve and Jackson Sinclair, the next few weeks surely served to prove them wrong. Eve had absolutely no contact with the man, although Lucie occasionally mentioned him in her letters. He had been in Boston one evening and Ted and Lucie had had dinner with him; he had arrived unannounced at Stonegate once when they had been spending the weekend there.

'It was all very cordial—quite pleasant, really,' Lucie had written, 'although I don't think he's really made up his mind yet about us. It's hard to keep waiting,' she had added wistfully, 'but I suppose we don't really have any choice. It would be so much easier if I didn't care about him!'

Easier for her if she didn't either, Eve found herself thinking, and was instantly furious with herself. It was that damned kiss—and, she was forced to admit, her reaction to it, which had put that thought in her mind. God alone knew why Jack had kissed her; it was probably because he'd felt like it at that moment, and a man like Jack Sinclair was accustomed to doing as he pleased.

For two months, she succeeded in forgetting about him remarkably well. Then, through no fault of her own, he disturbed her carefully constructed existence, and did so at a moment when she was poorly prepared to handle either him or herself.

It happened on the day she returned from a working trip to California, where she had spent nearly two weeks doing a number of fashion shoots and several product promotions. When she had finished the last of her assignments, late Saturday afternoon, she had been so anxious to get home that she had booked on the first available flight back to New York. Even an all-night flight and the change in time zones had seemed preferable to another night in a hotel-room, and all she could think of was the blessed relief of being back in her own apartment and her own bed.

But there hadn't been any great feeling of relief.

She should have known, Eve thought, her spirits sinking as she opened the apartment door and her senses were assaulted by what waited inside. This time, Jane's housekeeping lapses were worse than usual. In addition to the clutter and dust Eve had come to expect, she found the remains of a party strewn about both the living-room and the kitchen. Every conceivable surface was littered with empty glasses, overflowing ashtrays and platters of limp crackers and dried out cheese, and the final blow came when she found Jane's note posted under a magnet on the refrigerator door.

'Damn,' Eve said softly when she'd digested the note, and for a moment she felt like crying. Jane had blithely explained that she'd thrown a party on Friday night, following which she and a few of her friends had decided to take off for a weekend at the shore. 'There simply wasn't time to clean up before we left,' Jane had written without any attempt at an apology, and then had finished with the information that she would be back late Sunday evening. 'PS,' she had concluded with what Eve considered to be the ultimate injustice, 'there isn't any coffee left, so you'll have to go out and buy some.'

'Damn!' Eve said again, more loudly, and the words echoed in the empty apartment. This time Jane had gone too far! This time she could clean up after herself! *She* would have none of it, Eve resolved, too tired to control her anger. She turned her back on the mess, carried her suitcases into her bedroom and dropped them on the floor. Then, without bothering to unpack, she took a quick shower and fell into bed, instantly asleep.

When the door buzzer woke her, Eve groaned, cursing Jane for forgetting her key—and for getting back early, she realised, glancing at the clock. No wonder she didn't feel as though she'd had a decent sleep! It was only a little after two, and she'd counted on being left undisturbed until at least five or six.

'You might show a little consideration,' she began crossly as she opened the door—then stopped dead as she realised that it wasn't Jane. Instead, it was Jack, already taking in her tangled hair and cotton nightdress—and, she realised with a sinking feeling, the mess in the room beyond.

CHAPTER FOUR

'It must have been quite a party,' Jack observed with a brief expression of distaste, moving past her to enter the apartment without waiting for an invitation. He took another moment to survey the room and then turned back to her. 'You'd better put on a robe,' he said without emotion, but his close scrutiny reminded her that her nightdress didn't leave much to the imagination. 'Sorry to have disturbed you so early,' he added with sarcastic emphasis as she fled down the hall.

Something else to hold against Jane, Eve thought viciously, slamming the bedroom door behind her. It was obvious that he thought *she'd* thrown the wild party and had been up all night. He didn't like it either, she told herself as she hunted through her closet for a respectable robe. She'd just destroyed—no, *Jane* had just destroyed—whatever credibility she had managed to achieve. 'Damn her,' she said yet again, zipping up the robe she'd finally found, remembering that her slippers were packed at the bottom of one of her bags. Perhaps she could explain, she decided a little more calmly, and there was at least the consolation that Jack hadn't accused her of having a man in the bedroom with her! With those two thoughts in mind, she drew a deep breath and opened the bedroom door.

'Sorry about the mess,' she apologised as she re-entered the living-room to find Jack standing exactly where she had left him. 'You see, I just——'

'Explanations aren't necessary,' he said coldly, handing her an envelope. 'I've been away for a week, and I found this waiting for me when I got back this morning. What do you know about it?'

'I don't even know what it is,' she told him, completely confused, longing for a cup of coffee. 'I've been——'

'Then read it,' he snapped.

The envelope contained a handwritten letter from Lucie, heavily underscored and busy with repetitions. But when Eve had worked her way through it, the meaning—and the reason for Jack's anger—were clear.

The gist of it was that she and Ted had decided to be married in two weeks. 'I hope you won't be *too* angry,' Lucie had written. 'I know you hadn't made up your mind yet, and I know you've had reservations about us, but surely you've seen enough of Ted now to realise how good he is, and how right he is for me! Do try to understand, Jack—please? We just *can't* wait any longer, but we want you to be with us, and we don't want you to be angry. We've written Eve more about our plans, and I expect she can explain things better than I have.'

'Perhaps you would explain now,' said Jack when she finally looked up from the letter.

'But I don't know anything about it,' Eve said, her voice little more than a whisper. 'I haven't had a letter! I've——'

'Of course there's been a letter,' he snapped,

cutting her off again, just as she was about to explain that she'd been away. 'I expect there've been innumerable telephone calls as well. Was this your idea?' he demanded, then continued before she could even attempt an answer. 'It must have been! I was mad enough to explain my waiting game to you, and you obviously decided that you and your precious brother couldn't take the risk. God knows what I'm going to do now!'

He was in a towering rage, and a detached part of Eve's mind was surprised to see that he could lose control to quite such an extent. Even when thwarted, she would have expected him to react with the kind of icy self-control she had seen before. But this was very different, and so she waited silently, watching as he attempted to pace the crowded room. Like a caged lion, she thought absently.

'You must be enjoying this,' he resumed savagely. 'It's what you've wanted from the first—to bring me to my knees, to leave me with no choice but to accept this damnable scheme of yours!'

'I . . . ' Words failed her. There were so many injustices in what he'd said that she couldn't possibly rebut them all, nor, she knew, would he give her the chance.

'There's nothing to do but have this out with them,' he continued, still angry, but he had clearly come to a decision. 'We'll go up now to settle things.'

'Now?' she repeated, trying to understand. 'What do you mean—*we'll* go up now? *I've* got nothing to do with this!'

'You've got everything to do with this!' The way

he turned on her was enough to make her flinch. 'Get dressed, and pack something for tonight.'

'I'm not going anywhere with you,' she tried to tell him, but even to her ears the words lacked conviction.

'Yes, you are.' He turned away from her; she couldn't see his face, but his voice was now ominously controlled. 'I don't want to be in your company any more than you want to be in mine, but this is a family matter. If they're going to be married—and it appears that they are—then it's going to be done properly, and you certainly know more about planning a wedding than *I* do.'

'I don't,' she was reckless enough to say. 'I've never been married either.'

'You're a woman,' he retorted, as though that explained everything. 'Now, will you please do as I say and get ready? The sooner we leave, the sooner we'll be done.'

He'd said 'please', but this was no request. It was a command, and Eve had no choice but to obey. If she continued to refuse, she was afraid he might actually use physical force.

'All right,' she said, carefully edging by his large figure, heading towards the temporary sanctuary of her bedroom.

It took very few minutes to dress and switch a few necessary items from one suitcase to the smaller one she would take with her, but when she started back towards the living-room, suitcase in hand, she nearly collided with Jane at the kitchen door. 'You're back,' she said unnecessarily, and Jane nodded.

'It's raining, and the cottage leaked, so we gave

up. You're off again, I hear,' she continued, following Eve back into the living-room. 'No need to introduce us,' she added with a quick glance towards Jack. 'We did the honours ourselves. If you're not back tomorrow night, I'll call and cancel your appointments. Have fun!' she called after them with a complete lack of tact or awareness of the realities.

A different mood seemed to have come upon Jack, Eve discovered once they were in the car. Perhaps he regretted having lost control, and now he was silent. That sense of distance was back, and she knew there would be no reaching him, even if she'd wanted to try.

She felt battered—too much travelling, too little sleep, too much anger, too much . . . *everything*, she decided helplessly. By the time they boarded the private jet, she was past caring about anything. she refused the steward's offer of coffee—the coffee she would have given her life for a little while ago. Instead, she curled up in her seat and closed her eyes, ignoring Jack completely. He had to wake her when the plane landed, and again, an hour later, when they finally reached Stonegate.

Those were the only two times he spoke to her during the trip, and once they were inside the house he paused only briefly as a maid waited to show her to her room. 'I'll get hold of them now. We'll have dinner at,' he paused to consult his watch, 'at eight. That gives them two hours to get here. In the meantime, you may go to your room.'

Dismissed like a schoolgirl, she thought, watching as he turned away, experiencing the second urge to cry of the day. But she was much restored when she came downstairs two hours later—which was just as well, she told herself with a fleeting smile. The evening promised to be difficult in ways neither she nor Jack had expected. All the time she had been in her room, she had been listening for the sound of Ted and Lucie's arrival, but there had been nothing to disturb the silence.

'Things don't seem to be going according to plan,' she found herself saying as she entered the library and saw Jack. 'They're not here yet, are they?' she prompted when he didn't answer.

'Of course they're not here yet,' he answered shortly, turning away to pour her a sherry without bothering to ask if she wanted it. 'I haven't been able to reach them; there's no answer at either apartment. They planned this,' he added with bitter emphasis as he turned back with her drink.

'Do you really think so?' she queried brightly, taking great care, this time, not to touch his fingers as she accepted the glass. 'Are you sure I didn't put them up to this too?'

'Don't be clever, Eve,' he said sourly, regarding her over the rim of his glass. 'It doesn't become you.' He finished his drink and then set down the glass. 'What is it? A chance to get back at me for the things I said this afternoon?'

'Probably,' she admitted honestly. 'It seems *you* may be just as ill-tempered as you like, but I'm not even allowed to be clever!'

'I like you better when you aren't,' he admitted with a disarming smile which caught her completely by surprise. 'And I realise now that I wasn't very fair this afternoon. At the time, I was too angry to be fair.'

'Of course you were,' she agreed evenly. 'You'd just found out that you weren't going to get your way, and I don't believe that happens very often.'

'Is that what you really think?' he asked with a very different smile, one which was laced with irony.

'Of course,' she answered crossly. 'I expect you confine yourself to business, where you've got more power than anyone else.'

'I don't always confine myself to business,' he objected softly.

'But it can't be so very different,' she retorted, 'not when you've got women throwing themselves at your feet.'

'*You* haven't thrown yourself at my feet,' he pointed out.

'And never will!'

'As stubborn as Ted and Lucie, in fact—the three of you determined to see that I don't get my way.'

'But they're different,' Eve countered quickly. 'They're in love!'

'Let's eat,' he commanded, steering her towards the dining-room. 'It's possible you won't be quite so ill-tempered after a meal.'

He was probably right, she admitted, realising that she'd had nothing to eat since the previous evening, unless she counted the sweet roll and coffee she had had on the plane from California. It helped, too, when Jack turned the conversation to pleasantly impersonal topics. The combination of good food, good wine, and the easiness between them were all having an effect, although she wasn't sure which was contributing the most to her sense of well-being.

Jack excused himself at the end of the meal, sending her into the library alone while he went to his office to try again to reach Ted or Lucie. 'I won't be long,' he promised, and there was a teasing quality about his smile which left her feeling vaguely concerned.

Was it really wise to feel quite so comfortable in his presence? she wondered, staring distractedly down at the silver coffee service. She knew she wasn't thinking very clearly at the moment, but surely it was better—*safer*!—when they were angry with one another.

'Well, they're back,' he began abruptly when he returned, and she was relieved to see that he was clearly irritated. 'I found them at Lucie's. They'd been away for the weekend with friends—whatever that means,' he continued with an expression of distaste, ignoring the cup of coffee Eve was offering. 'They had no idea that I'd want to see them this soon—that's according to Lucie. She thought I'd still be thinking it over.' He turned away to pour himself a brandy, then drank it on the spot. 'Good God! They give me two weeks' warning about something like this, then expect I'll spend more than half of it thinking things over!'

'You're sounding like a Victorian father,' she told him, unable to repress a smile. 'This is getting to be a melodrama.'

'I know—you're right. It's just that I can't understand it,' he explained, throwing himself down on the couch beside her. 'I can't begin to understand what it's like—to be young and in love and determined to marry.'

'But you must know,' she objected. 'You were engaged once, years ago. Lucie told me about it, although I don't suppose it happened quite as many years ago as she seems to think.'

'Lucie occasionally says more than she should, and so do you,' Jack said firmly, but his smile removed any sting from his words. 'And without going into any more detail, let's just say that it's possible to be young and engaged without being madly in love.'

'Then you weren't broken-hearted?' Eve asked impulsively.

'No,' he answered shortly. 'Don't romanticise me, Eve. I'm not the type.'

'I know that,' she assured him earnestly. 'It's just that I assumed you once *were*, but I certainly didn't think you were still suffering from the rejection.'

'I'm not,' he agreed drily, turning to look at her for the first time, 'which has nothing to do with Lucie and Ted. They'll be here in the morning, so that we can make plans,' he continued, deliberately changing the subject. 'Lucie was pleased you came up with me. She seems to feel you can reason with me and provide a softening influence.'

'She's got that wrong, hasn't she?' asked Eve, amused by the idea. 'We do nothing but fight, and I'm forever saying what you don't want to hear.'

'No, Lucie's right. God knows why,' he added after a moment, reaching out one hand to brush a loose curl back from her cheek.

'But you're always angry with me,' she protested foolishly, because there was no anger now in the way the tips of his fingers were tracing the curve of her cheek. 'Aren't you?'

'No, but sometimes you make it hard not to be. I was furious with you this afternoon.' His hand reached her shoulder, compelling her towards him. 'You might have told me you'd been away for a week and that you'd been travelling all night.' He was kissing her now—her eyelids, her temple, her cheek, the corner of her mouth. 'That you weren't sleeping off last night's wild party,' he added after a moment. 'Why didn't you tell me, Eve?'

He was driving her mad with all these clever kisses, she thought, a sensation of promise and wild excitement already building within her. 'You wouldn't give me a chance,' she finally managed to say.

'That's never stopped you before,' he told her, and she could feel his smile against her cheek as she slipped her arms around his neck. 'What stopped you today?'

'That was different,' she protested weakly.

'How was it different?' he persisted, moulding her body against the hard line of his.

'I don't know.' She sighed, all semblance of coherence slipping away as his mouth finally closed over hers and her lips parted to accept him. She was gripping his shoulders, her body arching instinctively when his hands moved lightly over the curve of her breasts with a deliberate sensuality.

'We've got a problem, I think,' said Jack at last, his breathing nearly as uneven as hers, 'and we're not going to solve it tonight. Much as I might like to,' he added after a moment, his lips beginning to seek hers again, even while he kept her hands imprisoned between them. 'You're an enchantment,' he murmured, his lips like fire against her skin. 'So lovely . . . ' He kissed her again with a kind of savage and wild abandon, then released her hands. 'You'd better go to bed,' he told her with a twisted smile, 'before I forget to be wise!'

Having breakfast alone on the terrace in the clear light of a June morning, Eve could accept the fact that separating the two of them had been the only way to resolve the situation. Now she was relieved to know that Ted and Lucie would be arriving soon. After that, she decided vaguely, there would be safety in numbers, no further intimate and dangerous moments for her and Jack.

She finished her breakfast, poured herself a second cup of coffee and lazed in the sunshine while she admired the garden beyond the terrace.

In appearance, it had changed greatly since her first visit two months before. Now there were masses of flowers—a riot of reds and blues, pinks and yellows against the varied shades of green. At the far end of the central path was a small fountain, water jetting up from a large amphora, then falling gently into the small pool below. The sound of the water blended with the songs of birds, the occasional drone of a bee and the constant stirring of leaves by the light breeze which provided relief on what would otherwise have been a hot day.

She didn't hear the sound of the car; the first she knew that Ted and Lucie had arrived came when the door from the house flew open and they were suddenly upon her.

'Eve! I'm so glad you're here,' Lucie began nervously, hugging her briefly while Ted hung back, clearly wary and on guard. 'What do you think? Jack sounded *so* angry last night, but he said we had to come up to make plans—whatever that means. I'm terrified, to be honest. I just don't want a horrible row, but Ted and I can't *stand* to wait any longer. How do you think he's going to react?' she demanded, throwing herself down in the chair next to Eve.

'I—I'm not sure,' Eve stumbled, disorientated by this abrupt destruction of her peaceful solitude. For the first time she was finding Lucie's constant chatter difficult to handle. 'He certainly was angry,' she began again, then remembered one fragment of their bitter exchange in her apartment, 'but he did say something about planning a wedding.'

'*Did he?*' Lucie demanded. 'Oh, that's wonderful! Ted, did you hear that?' she appealed, gripping his hand and then turning back to Eve with a radiant smile. 'You're a love, and I knew you'd be able to soften him up and make him see reason!'

'I don't think you can say she's made me see reason,' Jack offered drily, materialising unexpectedly behind their circle of chairs, 'and you must know me well enough to realise that no one can change my mind for me—not even Eve.'

'But this means so much!' wailed Lucie, the anxious puppy look Eve remembered in evidence again. 'I don't want us to be fighting, or for you to be angry with me, or for——'

'Yes. I know what you don't want, and what you *do*,' he agreed, the firm note in his voice cowing her completely. 'You're both far too young; there are still far too many unanswered questions, and I fail to see the reason for such haste.'

'It's not what you might think, sir,' Ted said quickly, speaking for the first time and somehow managing to sound politely assertive. 'I'm afraid it's my work. We had intended to wait longer—until Christmas at least—but there's been a change in my schedule. My fieldwork will begin in September, instead of the spring, and I want to take Lucie with me——'

'I couldn't bear to stay behind,' Lucie interjected with passionate conviction.

'—but it wouldn't be suitable,' Ted continued evenly, ignoring his beloved's interruption, 'unless we're married. A year apart is a long time, sir.'

'Agreed,' Jack nodded, while Eve wondered where her brother had acquired the habit of inserting the deferential 'sir' in appropriate places. 'But if the two of you really love each other enough, you'll be able to wait the year.'

'I'm sure they'd be *able* to wait,' Eve found herself saying, even though she had been determined to keep still, 'but I don't see why they should be *forced* to. Nor will they be, for that matter. They don't need your permission; they want your approval, which is something entirely different. What Lucie doesn't want is an estrangement between you, and I don't think you want that either.'

'So you keep telling me,' Jack agreed quickly, 'but that's not all there is to consider. *I* wonder how well the two of you will get along when the novelty wears off.'

'Lucie and I have discussed that, sir, and I don't believe you need to worry,' Ted told him, showing considerably more poise than Eve would have expected. 'Neither of us sees marriage as an ending. It's a beginning, only a start. If two people really love each other as deeply as we do, they're prepared to make adjustments. We realise we're going to have to make any number of them.

'I won't be the easiest person to live with,' he continued, warming to the subject. 'I've already acquired a lot of—well, scholarly idiosyncrasies, I suppose. But Lucie's adaptable—she's had to be, hasn't she? Given the way her life has gone, it's been a necessity. And I've told her—so this isn't the first time she's heard this—that she . . . bubbles more than some men could stand. But I've spent so much time alone, or at least without anyone to be close to, that I *like* that warmth and enthusiasm in her.'

'Ah.' Jack sounded surprised. 'You've just addressed my two major reservations. Frankly, I don't believe I could stand either one of you on a long-term basis—much less a lifetime. But then there's no accounting for taste, is there?'

The others waited as he leaned back in his chair, studying Ted and his sister through narrowed eyes, while Eve covertly studied him. The sun was nearly overhead, its strong light playing strange tricks with his appearance. His hair seemed lighter than ever, but the way it slanted across his brow cast an oddly angled shadow on to his features. In the contrast of light and darkness, his eyes were an almost silvery grey and, at the moment, they seemed very far away, as though he had lost himself in intensely personal thoughts. Then, with an effort Eve could actually feel, he returned to the present.

'Well . . . ' he began, and in the silence before

he continued, the gentle murmur of the fountain was clearly audible. ' . . . it seems I have no choice—except to dictate the terms.'

'What terms?' Lucie, looking indignant, had opened her mouth to ask the question, but it was Ted who actually said the words.

'That you do this properly,' Jack explained dispassionately. 'There's bound to be a certain amount of talk, but most of it can be prevented if the conventions are observed. First,' he continued, finally looking up at them, 'I'll see that your engagement is properly announced, within the next week or two.'

'We're going to be married next weekend,' Lucie objected stubbornly. 'It's all planned.'

'What? The two of you and a justice of the peace?' Jack countered. 'And possibly Eve,' he added, his speculative gaze resting briefly on her. 'That won't do at all. You'll be married at the end of the summer. Here, I think,' he finished, looking out across the garden.

'Do you mean a formal wedding?' demanded Lucie. 'A *production*?'

'Hardly that,' he answered coolly, his eyes still on the garden. 'Something in good taste and properly done—the sort of thing that's expected.'

'But that's so much work,' Lucie pointed out, suddenly a little breathless, and Eve could see she was torn between that consideration and the romantic image of a garden wedding. 'I wouldn't know how to do it—where to start, what to plan . . . Unless Eve could help,' she added hopefully.

'Yes, use Eve if you like—and if she's willing,'

Jack agreed thoughtfully. 'Of course she's already pointed out that she knows nothing about weddings—never having been married. But she's got good taste and a sense of style.' Abruptly he got to his feet, and Eve sensed a change in his manner, a stiffness which probably meant he didn't like admitting that she had any good points. 'And there must be people one can hire to do this sort of thing,' he continued, clearly anxious to leave. 'I'll have someone look into the matter, find someone suitable. So long as the two of you are willing to agree to that, you have my approval, or blessing, or whatever it is you want—and my continued financial support, of course.'

'That was never a concern, sir,' Ted said firmly, already on his feet and looking directly at Jack. 'We never cared about that. We still don't.'

'I'm sure,' Jack agreed with the briefest of smiles, 'but it *will* help to make things more comfortable.' Then he finally did turn away, going back along the terrace until he disappeared around the corner of the house.

'So,' said Ted to Lucie, managing to sound both satisfied and indulgent, 'that went far better than you expected, didn't it?'

'I suppose so,' she agreed vaguely, still staring after Jack, her expression thoughtful. 'It went very well, but there's more to it than that.'

'What do you mean?' asked Ted, sitting down again and taking Lucie's hand in his.

'Well, I think we've opened a wound, in a strange sort of way. All that talk about doing things properly—it's because his own wedding got called off at the last minute. It couldn't have been easy for him, although he never let anyone see what he felt. He's always had too much pride for that, but it's as though he's got to make *our* wedding be all the things his never had a chance to be.'

'But you don't really mind, do you?' asked Ted with a teasing smile. 'I got the feeling that the idea of a formal wedding appealed to you.'

'Of course,' Lucie agreed almost absently, 'but it's sad to think he's still bothered by what happened all those years ago. At least there's Eve,' she continued obscurely, but the thought seemed to cheer her. 'He'd never have agreed to any of this if it hadn't been for Eve. I think he likes you,' she explained, focusing on Eve.

'I don't,' countered Eve. 'We're always fighting.'

'But he likes you all the same,' Lucie said firmly. 'I've never seen him like this before. You intrigue him, but he's fighting it.'

'That's nonsense,' Eve told her, now even more uncomfortable.

'No, I think Lucie's right,' offered Ted, taking up the argument. 'I've seen the way he looks at you, the way he watches you.'

'It's because you're not afraid of him,' Lucie explained. 'He likes to spar with you.'

'And I'm supposed to enjoy that?' asked Eve, trying for the right tone of ironic amusement. 'Being used as his sparring partner?'

'You know you do,' Ted told her. 'The two of you meet as equals, and there aren't many men you can say that about. I doubt if you've ever met one before.'

'I've certainly never met anyone quite like your

brother—no offence intended,' Eve said to Lucie, trying to turn the whole thing into a joke. 'He's far too domineering and autocratic for my taste.

CHAPTER FIVE

AFTER Eve's quelling pronouncement, Ted and Lucie apparently decided that there was no point in continuing to advance their theory about Jack. Besides, their own good fortune was still so deliciously new that it couldn't be ignored for long. Soon the two of them were so busy discussing their future together that they forgot everything else.

After lunch, at their insistence, Eve joined them at the swimming pool which lay beyond the garden, discreetly screened by high yew hedges. Since she had no bathing suit with her, she sat at the edge of the pool, watching Ted and Lucie as they played in the water like children. And why shouldn't they? she thought lazily. Their future was finally settled, no doubts remained, and they could revel in their good fortune. Some time soon, she supposed, she would have to begin to think about her own future.

But not today, she decided, getting up and starting away from the pool. She would think about the future some other day. For now, all she wanted was to be alone, to try to recapture the pleasant feeling of tranquillity she had been enjoying before Ted and Lucie had arrived. She slipped quietly through the opening in the yew hedge and took the shallow granite steps which brought her up to the rose beds at the side of the garden.

The morning's breeze had died, and the heat of a summer afternoon lay over the quiet garden, creating a kind of dreaming lassitude in her. She wandered slowly along the path, pausing occasionally to touch a bloom or to admire the arrangement of a particular bed. Here was a serenity that was almost protective, with no future to be faced, no decisions to be made, but with the freedom to allow her thoughts to drift as they pleased.

She wasn't sure how much time had passed when movement caught her eye and she glanced up to see Jack coming towards her from the direction of the house. 'You're thinking very hard about something,' he observed as he reached her side. 'I wonder what.'

'Nothing, really,' she explained easily. 'It's so peaceful here that I'm feeling happy and free. I can see why the first paradise was a garden. They're magic places, aren't they?'

'Yes,' he agreed, smiling down at her, 'and I don't know what could be more appropriate than finding Eve in the garden.'

'Thank you,' she said, then wondered if he had been complimenting her or merely making an observation. 'Thank you for what you've done,' she began again, 'for Ted and Lucie, for being willing——'

'For giving in without a fight?' he asked, beginning to walk slowly along the path while she kept step beside him. 'Or for agreeing to finance them so you won't have to?'

'You know I didn't mean that! That's never mattered.'

'I know it's never mattered to your brother.' He

paused briefly to look down at her. 'You were right about him,' he conceded. 'I've never met a young man with such a notable lack of concern as to how he and his intended were to be supported. Of course he's never had to worry about that—it's always been your problem, hasn't it? You've made life entirely too comfortable for him, you know, protected him from too many of the harsh realities.'

'Don't be unpleasant now,' she said impulsively, 'not when the day started out so well—when you made them so happy. And I think you'll be happier too.'

'I know.' He smiled, a brief and empty expression. 'Because I won't be so alone, I suppose. Did it ever occur to you that I might prefer to be alone?'

'No,' she answered frankly. 'I can't imagine anyone preferring to be alone. Making the best of the reality, perhaps, but not actively preferring it.'

'I wonder if you're right,' he mused, then deliberately changed the subject. 'Have you seen the knot garden yet?' he asked, and when she shook her head, he led the way down a side path. 'My grandmother planned the whole garden, but this is the only part I actually saw in progress. I remember watching, one day when I was very young, while she instructed the gardeners to root out what seemed to me to be perfectly acceptable rose bushes. When I asked her why, she showed me the plans she'd found for an old English knot garden and explained that it would take the place of the roses.'

He stopped by a small square plot, perhaps only ten feet to each side. Beyond a low box edging,

Eve saw even smaller box hedges, six or eight inches high and carefully trimmed to perfectly squared edges. The focal point of the little garden was a marble sculpture of a cherub, encircled by the hedge. From the circle, other hedges radiated outward with geometric precision, creating a design of diamonds and triangles. It was all in varying shades of green, with the contrasting pale pink of dwarf roses within each enclosed design.

'It's charming,' Eve told him, awed by its delicacy and by the thought of how much careful labour had gone into its making.

'Yes, and the only part of the garden I know much about,' he explained, staring down at the design, a faraway look in his eyes. 'I watched it take shape—it was several years until it began to look like this. I couldn't see the design at first, even though I'd looked at the plans. I remember telling my grandmother that it had been prettier before she had the roses torn out, that now all she had left was a bare spot and some weeds.

'She told me to be patient,' he continued with a reminiscent smile, 'that some day it would be lovely again. She said that gardens teach patience, and that if I learned nothing else from her, she hoped I'd learn that.'

'She sounds like a lovely person,' Eve said softly, fascinated by this small glimpse of Jack's childhood. 'She must have been, to have created all this.' Her gesture encompassed not only the knot garden, but everything around them. 'And it must have given her such pleasure,' she added almost wistfully.

'If it did, that was all she had,' he mused, the

faraway look back in his eyes. 'From the time my
father went away to school, she and my grandfather lived apart. Her life was centred here, and I
expect she was very lonely. These gardens seem to
have been her only passion, her only satisfaction.

'I remember what she told me once,' he went
on, and he seemed so caught up in memory that
Eve didn't think he knew precisely what he was
telling her. 'She said *my* mother ought to have a
garden of her own—that she wouldn't be unhappy,
that she wouldn't need so many distractions, if she
had a garden of her own. As though a garden
could be enough,' he finished abruptly, making an
obvious effort to shake off the memories.

'I'm the last in a long line of misogynists,' he
explained, a harder edge to his voice. 'You see the
ruins of my grandparents' marriage all around you,
but at least that marriage produced something
besides a son to carry on the family name. Things
didn't work out even that well for my parents. My
father never said so, but I think my mother's only
value to him was that she'd produced a son. He
didn't take any particular interest in her; he didn't
seem to care what she did, so long as she was
discreet.

'She had a great many—relationships, I suppose
you might call them,' he continued, while Eve
listened in amazement. 'I can't remember a time
when she wasn't trying to find someone to care, or
trying to believe that someone *did* care. For all I
know, Lucie is the result of one of those vain
attempts—not that I can blame my mother for
that, or care any less for Lucie. Perhaps she means
even more to me because of that possibility. She's

the only real link I have with my mother, whose greatest crime was that she wanted love. Unfortunately she made a habit of choosing men incapable of giving her what she wanted—first my father and then the others who came after. In my own case, my bride-to-be saw the writing on the wall and beat a hasty and prudent retreat just in time. She's been married to someone else for at least ten years, and she's surely happier than she would have been if she'd married me. Perhaps now you can understand why I've been so sceptical of this grand romance between your brother and Lucie,' he explained, turning to address her for the first time. 'It really had very little to do with what I might think of Ted, or of you, for that matter. It's simply that this sort of thing—I suppose you call it love— is completely beyond my understanding. You were right, Eve. I *am* a hard man, and I don't pretend to understand the concept of love. I'm third generation hard,' he told her with a smile of mocking amusement, 'and there's been no love in this family to understand for at least that long. You ought to remember that,' he ended suddenly, turning away to walk rapidly back to the house.

Without the presence of Ted and Lucie to keep the conversation going, dinner would have been a grim and silent affair. They were too happy to notice anything, but Eve was very aware that Jack had almost nothing to say. He sat at the head of the table, withdrawn—even brooding, she thought— yet every time she risked a glance in his direction, she found him watching her. But why? she wondered, her mind worrying at the problem even while she tried to hold up her end of a discussion of wedding plans. He certainly wasn't watching her in the way Ted had suggested he did. There was nothing in his expression to suggest promise or excitement or anticipation of the future. Perhaps he was displeased to have revealed so much of himself, or afraid that she wouldn't heed his warning. It was asking too much to believe that he might be regretting the warning itself, although that was what she wanted to believe.

'Eve, will you?' Lucie was asking, forcing Eve to return to the present.

'If you like,' she agreed automatically, having no idea what she'd agreed to, only hoping that her lack of attention hadn't been noticed. 'It's up to you—whatever you want,' she added for good measure.

'Of course I want you! We both do,' Lucie assured her with affectionate intensity. 'After all you've done to help, I couldn't possibly have anyone else as maid of honour.'

Heavens! thought Eve, biting back her instinctive protest as she realised just what Lucie had in mind. At most, she had been imagining herself serving as a surrogate mother of the groom—a self-effacing and inconspicuous one at that. 'Are you sure?' she asked doubtfully.

'Of course,' Lucie affirmed again, then appealed to Jack, 'I'm right, aren't I? This wouldn't be happening—at least not as nicely and happily—if Eve hadn't gotten through to you!'

'I expect you're right,' he agreed easily enough, as though he'd been following the discussion closely. 'She has amazing powers of persuasion.'

'You see?' said Lucie, turning to smile radiantly up at Ted. 'Everything's falling into place, and it's going to be perfect.'

'Of course it is,' Ted agreed with the air of a man very much in love, prepared to agree to anything his intended said.

'Well, that's everything,' Lucie concluded comfortably, displaying what Eve considered to be a lamentable lack of understanding of the work involved in planning a wedding. 'You wouldn't mind if we went out for a while, would you?' she asked, addressing her question to both Jack and Eve.

'I don't see why,' Jack answered more naturally. They had long since finished dinner and had been lingering at the table while Lucie outlined her plans. 'I expect the two of you would like to be alone.' He stood up, watching silently until Ted and Lucie had left the room before he turned to Eve. 'I've got some calls to make. You'll excuse me?'

'Of course,' Eve agreed automatically, but she was speaking to his back, because he had already started for his office. What else had she expected? she asked herself, feeling slightly deflated.

She read for a while in her room and then, because it was still early and she was unaccountably restless, she decided to go out for a walk. She would have liked to go back to the knot garden, but that was too near the office wing. Since Jack clearly didn't want her presence, she turned left when she crossed the terrace, heading towards the loggia which overlooked the pond.

There was a bench at the far end, and she sat

there for a long time, watching the way the
moonlight reflected off the waters of the pond, her
face lifted to the cooler evening breeze. Once she
looked back at the house, studying the random
pattern of lighted windows, particularly those of
Jack's office. Perhaps she was only imagining it,
but she thought she could see the ghost of a
shadow at one of the windows—Jack working at
his desk, she supposed. Then she forced herself to
turn away again.

You're a fool! she scolded. To be thinking the
kinds of thoughts she was tonight was madness. It
was just physical attraction—much as she hated to
admit that fact!—and the mystique of the man. He
was, after all, larger than life in every sense of the
word, and it would take a woman of considerably
more sophistication than she not to be attracted to
him.

Someone—probably one of the maids—had been
through the house, turning off lights. Now the
windows were dark, except those of the central
hallway and Jack's office. As she climbed the steps
to the terrace, she entered deep shadows, but when
she turned back to look once more at the garden
she saw that it was bathed in the light of a rising
moon. The daytime riot of colours had been
reduced to varying shades of grey, but the mingled
fragrances of roses and lavender were heavy on the
air of this quiet night. She took a deep breath,
savouring the magic of the moment, then started
as she heard a small sound behind her.

'Taking one last look at the ruins?' She turned
to see Jack detach himself from the shadows beside
the house and come to stand next to her at the top

of the steps. 'Lucie wants to be married out there,' he mused, staring off across the moonlit garden. 'I find that ironic, although I suppose you're a romantic, aren't you, Eve?'

'Yes,' she answered honestly, 'although I sometimes wonder why.'

'What's the matter? Don't you have many opportunities to put your romantic impulses to work? No men madly in love with you?'

'None, given the world I live in,' she explained uneasily, wondering what he was getting at. 'The men I meet are either interested only in what they can get out of a relationship, or . . . '

'Not interested in you at all,' he suggested helpfully. He hesitated briefly. 'I don't suppose you'd join me for a drink, would you?'

'I don't think——' she began uncertainly, but he cut her off.

'Why not? It's early yet.'

'All right,' she agreed, giving in when she knew it would have been wiser not to. But there had been something in his voice—almost a note of appeal, she thought—which had persuaded her.

Quite impersonally, he took her arm to guide her along the dark terrace and around the corner to his office. Inside, the lamp on his desk cast only a small circle of light, reducing most of the room to shadows.

Was this how he spent his evenings, his nights? she wondered, looking slowly around while he poured their drinks. The thought saddened her, just as she had been saddened by the things he had told her this afternoon.

'Shall we drink to the happy bride and groom?'

he asked, handing her one glass and raising the other one briefly to her. 'Lord, they're so young,' he mused after he had taken a sip, 'and it's so easy to think you're in love at that age.'

'It's easy to be in love, when you've found the right person,' Eve suggested carefully. They were facing each other, standing in the centre of the room beyond the pool of light from the desk, but she could still see his quick smile. 'You don't agree, of course.'

'Of course. You're the romantic, not I,' he answered with another smile, 'and the conceit of the young never ceases to amaze me.'

'What do you mean?'

'They're so sure of themselves.' He paused to finish his drink and then turned to set his glass down on the edge of the desk. 'It's as you get older that the doubts begin to set in. By the time you're my age, that's all you have left.'

'You shouldn't say that,' she protested. 'You make yourself sound positively ancient!'

'I *am* positively ancient—at least I feel that way. Nine years older than you, in fact. Turn around,' he added.

The command was so unexpected that Eve obeyed without thinking. 'What are you doing?' she asked, uncertain, as she felt his hands in her hair.

'Taking out the pins,' he explained almost absently, his fingers busy at the task, dropping each pin carelessly to the floor. 'There, that's better.' He spent a few seconds threading his fingers through her hair, then caught her lightly by the shoulders and turned her around to face him again.

'Much better.' He nodded, and her heart skipped a beat as she saw the way he was looking at her. 'You shouldn't wear it up,' he told her, his hands on her shoulders holding her captive. 'Particularly when you're in a garden, your hair ought to be free—all tumbled around your face. There's no use being Eve in the garden if you don't look the part. But you tempted me all the same.' His hands left her shoulders to catch her by the waist. 'You still do,' he added softly, pulling her against him as his lips first touched hers.

There was something very deliberate—almost calculating—about the way he was kissing her, and Eve realised it immediately. His tongue was tracing the line of her mouth, but when her lips parted, she sensed his slight withdrawal, even as he continued his clever teasing. This was the kind of kiss which had nothing to do with how he felt about her, and everything to do with how he wanted *her* to feel. She knew that, but knowledge was no defence against the act.

Jack was making her want more than he was willing to give. She could feel her body melting against the hard line of his, and she wrapped her arms around his neck, trying to pull him even closer. 'Please,' she whispered in something close to a sigh, and felt him withdraw even more.

'Do I tempt you too?' he asked, although he already knew the answer. He could feel her response, could feel the way her body was coming alive, moving against his with a kind of sensual grace, but that wasn't enough for him. 'Say it,' he commanded, his teeth gently catching her lower lip, then instantly releasing it.

'Yes, you know you do,' she whispered, instantly rewarded as his mouth closed over hers with fierce authority, scattering her thoughts as she gave herself up to the slow spiral of desire he was creating within her.

'I want you,' he murmured some time later, when his lips had finally left hers, his fingers working with the zipper at the back of her dress until he could part it. 'God, how I want you!'

His touch was a fire against her skin, one infinitely protracted caress as he slipped her dress from her shoulders. She stood motionless, with no defences left, as he discarded it completely and then lowered his head so that his lips could trace the curve of her breast. It was all sensation now, his hands and his lips inflaming her even further, while she fumbled with the buttons of his shirt. By the time she finally had them all, his breathing was as uneven as her own.

'That's right,' he murmured unsteadily as she began her own tentative explorations. 'Yes . . . lord, that's wonderful!' She could feel the muscles contracting beneath her touch as his mouth closed hungrily over hers, his own control now as thoroughly shattered as hers. Their kiss was an acknowledgment of mutual need and desire, but she knew it wasn't enough for either of them. They wanted so much more—they wanted everything, she realised, gladly permitting him to draw her back with him until they lay together on the couch, his body covering hers. 'Wonderful,' he said again, his lips returning to her breast when her hands dared to grow bolder. 'We're good together, Eve,' he breathed as she began to learn the power she had to excite him as much as he was exciting her. 'So good!'

Jack was her only reality now, desire a compelling force which absorbed her so completely that at first she could not comprehend the small sounds which nagged at her consciousness. Only slowly did she realise she was hearing footsteps in the central hall, Lucie's light laughter and the quiet murmur of Ted's voice.

'No! Please, Jack,' she whispered fiercely, struggling to free herself from his embrace. 'We can't!'

'Of course we can,' he contradicted absently, his hands and his lips still busy against her skin.

'They'll see us!'

'No, they won't,' he told her, raising his head to smile down at her. 'No one comes here unless they're told to.' Then his mouth closed over hers, his leisurely kiss effectively silencing any further protest from her until the house was silent again. 'You see?' he teased when his lips finally left hers. 'They're gone now.'

'That doesn't matter,' she told him, knowing that—for her, at least—the spell was broken, the madness over. 'We can't *do* this!'

'Of course we can,' he murmured, his lips trailing lightly down to her breast again. 'We're doing it, Eve.'

'No!' She twisted away from him, her hands against his shoulders, trying to hold him off. Suddenly everything was clear. He had told her she tempted him, had said they were good together, but he had never mentioned love—and never would, she realised bleakly. 'This doesn't mean anything to you!'

'It doesn't mean marriage, if that's what you're talking about,' he said, a sudden reserve in his voice. 'But you already knew that.'

'I'm not talking about marriage,' she flared indignantly. 'I'm talking about love!'

'Whatever that may be,' he shot back sarcastically, increasing the distance between them. 'For God's sake, Eve, don't ask more of me than I can give!'

'Then don't ask more of *me* than *I* can give!'

He swore softly under his breath, and she was forced to suffer the indignity of his sour look as she stood up and reached for her dress. 'You might have thought of that before you allowed yourself to get quite so carried away,' he said coolly. 'I've made it very clear to you exactly how things stand.'

'Perhaps I didn't believe you,' she snapped. 'Perhaps I thought there was more!'

'There isn't!' As she pulled on her dress and struggled with the zipper, he got up from the couch and crossed the room to pour himself a drink. 'I was as honest with you as I know how to be,' he resumed wearily. 'I've never been this honest with any other woman. If that's not enough, I don't know what is.'

'You should now,' she said evenly, because control was the only way to get through these last few seconds. 'I just told you. All I ask is love, and if that's more than you can give, find some other woman to *tempt* you and be *good* with you! My price is higher than that.'

'Obviously,' he agreed without expression, taking a swallow of his drink and then turning away as she left the room.

CHAPTER SIX

DEAR GOD, she'd been such a fool, Eve admitted bleakly, lying awake through a night that seemed endless. She had never been in love before, but she knew enough to understand that love couldn't exist in a vacuum. Loving was a part of being loved, and Jack had made it painfully clear that he wasn't going to love anyone. Yet she had allowed those moments in his office to happen; she had done more than allow them to happen, she corrected with painful honesty. There had been nothing passive about her behaviour. She had been unbelievably bold, so caught up in that entirely new world of passion and desire that she hadn't possessed a shred of self-control.

She turned her flushed face into the coolness of the pillow, remembering the way Jack's lips had teased at hers until she had been consumed by a wild and mindless wanting. The instincts of a lifetime hadn't been enough to save her; it was only the stiff dose of reality provided by Ted and Lucie's return to the house which had finally brought her to her senses.

At least there was that to be thankful for, she told herself, wondering why she felt no relief, no gratitude. Instead, there was only a kind of empty bitterness within her.

*   *   *

Towards dawn, she fell asleep, and felt like death when she awoke a few hours later. She procrastinated endlessly over her bath, her hair, her make-up and her clothes, until there was finally nothing to do but leave her room and force herself to go downstairs. She dreaded the thought of having to face Jack again, and she stopped dead in the doorway to the dining-room when she realised that the moment was already upon her. He was alone at the table, a cup in his hand and the morning paper spread out before him. She couldn't even turn and run, hoping he hadn't seen her, because he had already set down his cup and closed the paper.

'Don't hover, Eve,' he commanded, getting up to hold a chair for her, leaving her with no choice but to enter the room and sit down. 'The coffee's fresh,' he told her, taking his place again and pushing the paper aside. 'Would you like some?'

'Please.' She watched his hands while he poured for her, afraid to meet his eyes.

'Would you like breakfast now?' he asked, holding out the cup to her.

'No, thank you,' she answered, taking the cup from him very carefully, making sure that their hands didn't touch. She set it down in front of her, transferring her gaze from his hands to the delicate design on the saucer.

'Apparently it's your turn to be Victorian,' he observed after a moment, his voice touched by faint amusement, 'but it really won't do. It's uncharacteristic, Eve.'

'So was last night,' she was stung to reply.

'Obviously,' he agreed drily, 'but you might try

putting it behind you. It's the only reasonable thing
to do.'

'Reasonable?' she repeated with a certain bitter
wonder. 'Do you really think last night is the sort
of thing a person can be *reasonable* about?'

'Of course, but then I don't suppose I look at
these things as you do. What you consider a lapse
is merely a pleasant diversion to me. It doesn't
mean a thing.'

'God, you *are* cool, aren't you?' she demanded,
forgetting herself as she looked up to meet his
gaze.

'Yes.' His dark grey eyes held hers. 'I don't
know why you should be surprised; you've taken
every possible opportunity to point that out to
me.' Remarkably, he smiled. 'That's better, Eve.
You're getting your temper back, and it's a great
improvement!

'Look,' he continued—still being reasonable, she
thought resentfully, 'you'll save yourself all kinds
of trouble if you can continue to be angry with
me. What do you think my sister and your brother
will make of things if they come down to find you
playing the Victorian maiden? Painful blushes and
averted eyes aren't your style, and they're bound
to want to know what's brought them on. We've
got a wedding to get through; we're going to have
to spend at least a limited amount of time in each
other's company, and I don't see any reason why
we shouldn't behave towards each other as we
always have.'

'No, you wouldn't!'

'It will make things easier for Lucie and your
brother,' he continued, ignoring her comment.

'You're the one who's been so determined that they have a happy ending. What's the point of distracting them from their single-minded pursuit of wedded bliss? It really would be so much simpler and more pleasant to pretend it never happened.'

'More your style too,' Eve retaliated, hating him for being so cool about something she couldn't dismiss so easily.

Jack agreed with an ironic smile. 'That's very good, Eve. Just keep it up and we shouldn't have any problems.'

Perhaps he'd been right, Eve conceded at the end of the day, after she had returned to New York, fielded Jane's inevitable questions, and finally retreated to the privacy of her room. Certainly anger and resentment were more comfortable emotions than the confusion and embarrassment she'd felt when she had first joined him that morning. Safer too, she reminded herself.

Anger was definitely the best approach, she concluded over the next few days—that and plenty of hard work. While she had been at Stonegate, she had managed a private moment with Ted, and had written him an enormous cheque. 'It's to buy Lucie a ring,' she had explained, and at that moment she had been motivated by pride. She could imagine the minute diamond Ted would buy if left to his own devices! 'I want you to go to a really good jeweller,' she had insisted. 'Choose something substantial. Lucie's accustomed to nice things, and I don't want her to have to apologise for the ring you give her.'

'Lucie wouldn't do that,' Ted said, so carefully

that Eve instantly realised that she had overstepped.

'No, I know she wouldn't, and I shouldn't even have said it,' she apologised quickly. 'But wouldn't you like her to have something that's really lovely, something she can cherish?'

'Not when I'm spending your money,' countered Ted, trying to hand the cheque back to her.

'You're about to be independent of me, and it would be nice if you'd indulge me this one last time. Please?' Eve asked when he wavered. 'You might finally buy yourself some new clothes while you're at it, and don't worry about how much things cost! We're all going to be more comfortable now.'

Which was true enough, she reflected, but she wouldn't feel really comfortable until she'd built up her savings again. Accordingly, she had asked her agency for as much work as possible, and she was feeling rushed to death within just a few days. In addition to the work which had already been scheduled for her, she was trying to get as much more as she could. This necessitated 'go-sees', those difficult meetings between the prospective model and those connected with the intended ad campaign.

Eve hated them because they were really nothing more than the process of selling herself and then waiting to see if she would be bought. There was a lot of effort involved in dressing and doing her make-up and hair to attempt to suit the image she thought was wanted, and then she had to endure the humiliation of being inspected from every angle. Finally would come the nervous time of waiting while people looked through her book—the leather-bound portfolio which held representative photos and samples of her work.

Usually the result was a polite rejection, yet go-sees were a necessary evil, the best way to find new work, and Eve steeled herself to do all the agency could arrange for her. She landed a satisfying amount of new work in consequence, and was kept very busy during the rest of the summer.

The only break in her routine came during Lucie's five-day visit to New York to shop and make plans for the wedding. Eve had agreed to accompany her on her shopping expeditions and to offer advice, and she was looking forward to those days until she discovered that she was expected to stay all the time with Lucie—in Jack's apartment.

'It makes perfect sense,' Lucie explained. 'The bridal consultant Jack arranged to hire to help me will be meeting me there every morning, and there's no reason why you should have to meet us somewhere else. Besides, I'll only rattle around in Jack's place if you don't stay with me. He's in Singapore or Manila, or somewhere like that, and I *hate* being alone!'

'Oh, well, if he's going to be gone,' Eve had almost said—which wouldn't have done at all. Instead, she had meekly agreed, then wished she had found a way to refuse.

Jack's place—if, indeed, such a mundane word could be used to describe such an extraordinary penthouse—came as an unpleasant surprise. The place had undeniable elegance and style, but it had neither warmth nor personality. It wasn't a home; it seemed merely a decorator's showcase—agres-

sively severe, with neutral colours and furnishings
which seemed designed only to provide the proper
setting for what Eve considered to be a remarkably
cold and impersonal collection of modern paintings
and pieces of sculpture. The only life and colour
were provided by the view of the city's skyline
from the huge floor-to-ceiling windows that
dominated every room.

'You don't like this place, do you?' Lucie
remarked one evening, displaying a surprising
degree of perception. 'I've noticed it. You're happy
enough during the day, while we're out shopping,
but you're uneasy here.'

'It can't be that bad,' protested Eve, wishing she
had done a better job of hiding her feelings. 'It's
just that I don't like places that are quite this
modern.'

'Or is it that you don't like the idea that Jack
lives in a place that's quite this modern and stark?'

'Why should that matter to me?' Eve countered,
feigning a lack of concern. 'It's no business of mine
how Jack wants to live.'

'True,' Lucie agreed casually—almost too
casually, Eve thought, 'but I wondered if you
found it just a little depressing. I've always thought
this place shows the worst side of him. It's cold
and rather hard—and Jack can be both of those,
of course. But that's not all he is, and I'd hate to
have you be so influenced by this place that you
forgot how much more there is to him than you
see here.'

'As far as I'm concerned, Jack *is* cold and hard,'
Eve said, clear warning in her voice, 'and I hope
you're not still trying to promote some kind of

thing between the two of us!'

'Well . . . ' The younger girl shifted uneasily. 'Not so much promoting as wishing,' she continued with a rueful smile. 'Ted and I have been talking about it, and both of us think you and Jack really do seem ideal for each other.'

'But we're not,' Eve said evenly, before Lucie could go any further. 'There's no point in thinking about it, because the two of us simply don't get along—and we never will,' she finished more firmly—which was, after all, no more than the truth.

Lucie took the hint then and Eve was relieved that she didn't bring it up again. By the end of the week most of the decisions had been made, and a designer had begun the task of creating Lucie's wedding gown, as well as Eve's dress and those of the two bridesmaids. Lucie went back to Boston and Eve returned to her busy schedule.

She hadn't expected to either hear from or see Jack until the weekend of the wedding, so it came as a complete surprise when he made contact late one Friday afternoon in early September. She had endured a particularly long and frustrating day, it was nearly seven, and she was physically exhausted and mentally drained. That was undoubtedly why she put up absolutely no resistance when she emerged from the studio to find a uniformed chauffeur waiting to present her with a note from Jack.

Less a note than a summons, she reflected as she read the precise and angular handwriting on the impressive headed stationery. He wanted a few minutes of her time; it would have to be this evening because he was leaving town in the morning, and she was to come to his office immediately. Without really thinking about it, she had nodded to the chauffeur and allowed him to relieve her of her tote bag before he installed her in solitary splendour in the rear of the limousine.

When they reached the modern skyscraper which housed Sinclair Enterprises, the chauffeur escorted her into the deserted lobby, where an earnest young man was waiting for her.

'Miss Foster,' he began, and Eve realised she was being eyed with a certain degree of well-bred curiosity. 'If you'll come with me, please. Mr Sinclair is expecting you.'

The executive offices of Sinclair Enterprises occupied all the sixty-first floor, and the reception area seemed vaguely familiar to her, although she had never been here before. Then she realised there was hardly any difference between the decorating scheme here and the one in Jack's penthouse.

The similarities depressed her, and she became even more depressed when she caught a glimpse of herself, reflected in one of the floor-to-ceiling windows. Now she understood why the young man had looked at her so strangely. At the moment, her appearance shrieked 'model!' to the world— trendy little dress of wild geometric print, hair a tumble of casual curls and confusion, artful make-up which emphasised the definition of her features, and the false eyelashes which she sometimes thought were a model's one indispensable item.

Damn! she said silently, wishing she hadn't been in such a rush to leave the photographer's studio. If she'd only taken the extra time necessary to remove her make-up and tame her hair! But she'd been so tired and anxious to get home, and she hadn't known her appearance was going to matter.

'In here, please,' the young man directed, opening one of the double doors ahead of them, indicating that she should enter. 'Mr Sinclair will be with you in a moment.' Then he closed the door, leaving her alone in an empty room.

She supposed it was Jack's office. It was certainly large enough to be the office of *the* Sinclair of Sinclair Enterprises, and it also looked for all the world like a room in his penthouse—the same neutral colours and furnishings, the same meaningless paintings and pieces of sculpture. The only new note was struck by an enormous teakwood desk by one wall of windows.

'It took you long enough to get here.'

'I just finished work.' She answered automatically, even before she turned towards the door and saw him. Immediately, she felt the need to be on guard. Tonight he seemed—if such a thing were possible—even more attractive than usual. He was wearing one of the pinstripe suits which apparently were his business uniform, but he had shed the jacket and loosened his tie. In his shirtsleeves, with the waistcoat still buttoned, the long line of his body was emphasised and his shoulders seemed even broader. He also seemed more vulnerable, with his hair slightly disordered, as though he had run his hand through it more than once in a gesture of impatience or frustration. The faint lines in his face were also more sharply incised—suggesting that his day had been just as bad as hers, Eve decided. Then she instantly repressed that thought and went on the offensive. 'If your spies were able to find me, they ought to have been able to tell you I was working!'

'Sorry to disappoint you, but there weren't any spies—just an efficient secretary.' Jack crossed the room to lean against the front of his desk, and Eve took the opportunity to study him as carefully as he was studying her. The strong light from above cast strange shadows over his features, making him appear even more tired, but she refused to feel any sympathy—particularly when he spoke again. 'You're obviously on your way out for the evening,' he observed, 'but you needn't worry, I won't keep you long. Sit down,' he commanded, indicating the nearest chair.

'Thank you,' she acknowledged evenly, although it rankled that he should make what was an admittedly logical mistake.

'I happened to be in Boston yesterday,' he resumed, 'and I had dinner with Lucie and your brother. I think it's only fair to warn you that I got the distinct impression that my sister is prepared to do a little subtle matchmaking.'

'I know,' Eve told him. 'She tried the same thing on me about two months ago.'

'Did she?' he asked, his tone less than pleasant. 'Are you sure it wasn't a suggestion *you* made—however indirectly?'

'A suggestion *I* made?' she demanded, flaring instantly at the idea that he should even think such a thing. 'You can't possibly believe that! Not after——' She stumbled briefly. 'Not after the way things ended between us the last time. Or is it that you think I'm looking out for the main chance after all?' she hurried on, rage permitting her to regain her stride. 'Do you think I decided that it's not enough to have my brother marry for money? Do you think I've decided to try to marry for even more?'

'The thought had occurred to me,' he agreed with what was probably deceptive mildness. 'It didn't seem beyond the realms of possibility that you might decide I was capable of a change of heart.'

'You haven't *got* a heart!'

Jack nodded approvingly. 'I was wrong, then, wasn't I?'

'Damn right!' she snapped, glaring at the unrevealing line of his back.

'Then I won't need to worry that you'll be constantly throwing yourself at me?'

'I have *never*——' Eve got no further as the telephone console on his desk buzzed softly, forcing her to wait. During the few moments while he listened to the caller, all her anger evaporated, replaced by an odd emotion which was somewhere between depression and a feeling of betrayal.

'Yes, tell them I'll be ready soon,' he said into the receiver just before he replaced it, and Eve was already on her feet by the time he turned back to her.

'You have people waiting for you,' she told him, suddenly wanting nothing so much as to get away from him. 'I'll leave now—unless there's something else.'

'There isn't,' he said, dismissing her coolly, watching as she crossed the room to the door. 'You shouldn't have spent so much for Lucie's ring,' he called after her when her hand was already on the knob.

'What's that supposed to mean?' she demanded fiercely, forgetting herself completely as she turned back to face him.

'She showed it to me last evening,' he explained without expression. 'It's very nice, but it's more than you can afford.'

'And of course you know that,' she raged. 'What is it? Does your private detective give you a daily report on my bank balance?'

'Of course not!' For the first time it sounded as though she'd got to him. 'But I've got a pretty good idea what it cost, and I don't like to see you spending so much. You might give a little thought to yourself.'

'And you, Mr Sinclair, might keep your nose out of my business!' Eve wrenched the door open, then slammed it behind her so hard that the sound echoed through the silent reception area. Only then did she see the four men waiting just beyond her, all of them eyeing her with a mixture of surprise and curiosity. Not that she cared, she told herself, squaring her shoulders and walking past them without a second glance. Let *him* explain why a tousled blonde wearing too much make-up had stormed out of his office and slammed the door in his face!

CHAPTER SEVEN

EVE spent the next two weeks trying to cultivate a little detachment of her own, enough to see her through whatever contact she and Jack would have during the weekend of the wedding. What she really wanted, in fact, was to feel nothing at all when she faced him. To that end, she worked at disciplining her emotions until she had managed to convince herself that whatever it was she had felt for Jack was over now.

She was wrong, of course, and it took no more than her first brief encounter with him to discover just how mistaken she had been. She had joined Lucie at Stonegate the Thursday before the wedding and managed to spend twenty-four hours in what she would always consider to be Jack's real home without any difficulty at all. But that was only because he hadn't arrived yet, as she discovered the next afternoon. She had been coming quickly down the stairs, not looking where she was going, and had suddenly found herself face to face with him. Even though they didn't actually collide, she felt as though the breath had been knocked out of her as she looked up at him.

'What are you doing here *now*?' she demanded fiercely, all the colour draining from her face and then surging back in a vivid flush. 'You're not supposed to be here yet,' she told him, her voice trembling slightly. He wasn't supposed to arrive until evening, she thought, resenting the fact that she'd been given no warning. It wasn't fair that he should appear so soon, and she was painfully aware that the silence between them was lengthening uncomfortably. 'You're coming later,' she added foolishly. 'Aren't you?'

'I got away a little sooner than expected,' he explained without expression in his voice, but there was a careful, guarded quality in the way he was looking at her. 'Perhaps it's just as well that I did. I've already been told that Lucie's a mass of nerves at the moment, afraid that I won't be back in time, and that she'll have to walk down the aisle alone.'

'Yes, she's been worrying about that,' Eve agreed awkwardly, 'but then she's been worrying about nearly everything today. I—I think all brides are like that.' She was stammering like a schoolgirl—and blushing like one too, she realised, wishing a hole would open in the floor and swallow her. 'It's—it's natural, I suppose.'

'I'm sure,' Jack said coolly, dismissing her stumbling attempts at polite conversation, 'and I'll just go up and let her know that I *have* come in time to give her away.'

Was it always going to be this difficult? she wondered, staring after him as he moved past her and started up the stairs. When he was out of sight, she found that her legs didn't want to support her, and sank down on the nearest chair, lacing her fingers together to control their trembling. She'd forgotten, she realised, feeling dazed. She'd forgotten everything—how large he was, how attractive—how attracted to him she was, she admitted, wishing there was some way to eliminate *that* from her mind. She would never be able to behave with any semblance of composure in front of him, she told herself, suddenly feeling a little sick. The wedding—this whole weekend—was going to be absolute and utter hell; people were going to notice that there was something definitely odd about her every time she had to look at Jack or speak to him. *Jack* would notice too, which was the worst thought of all.

But if he did, he gave no sign. He kept as much distance between them as possible, speaking to her only when it couldn't be avoided. At those times, he behaved towards her with completely impersonal politeness, as though she were a stranger whose acquaintance he had only recently made. That approach steadied her and helped her to regain her poise. It made it possible for her to speak to him without making an utter fool of herself, but it hadn't been easy.

But all that had been forgotten by the time the wedding was about to begin. For the first time since she had seen him the previous day, Eve wasn't thinking of Jack. She and Lucie's two bridesmaids were waiting for their musical cue, standing just inside the door leading to the terrace, and Eve's breath caught at the beauty of the scene before her.

All day it had been sunny and warm, more like June than mid-September. Now the rays of the afternoon sun slanted across the roof of the house, illuminating all the colours of the garden with golden radiance. The air was still heavy with the fragrance of roses, and the gentle murmur of the

fountain mingled with the songs of the birds and
the strains of Bach from the string quartet
positioned in the loggia.

Ahead, beyond the even rows of guests, Eve
could see Ted, standing between his best man and
the minister. He looked so grown up, she thought
with surprise. In his formal clothes he was no
longer the boy he had always been to her. He was
actually a handsome man, she realised, standing
tall and ramrod-straight, the sun turning his light
brown hair to a fairer shade.

And Lucie, waiting just behind her on Jack's
arm, was as lovely as every bride should be. Her
dark hair and vivid colouring were a perfect foil
for the creamy white of the organza and silk gown.
The designer touches showed in the little cap
sleeves, in the graceful curve of the neckline, and
in the way the full skirt fell into gentle folds from
the broad silk sash which emphasised her slender
waist. Creamy white roses from the garden had
been woven into her hair, and she carried a simple
bouquet of the same flowers.

The bridesmaids' gowns were of a deep yellow,
while Eve's was an arresting shade of rusty
orange—both colours she associated with the most
melancholy aspects of autumn. But there was
nothing melancholy about this day, she thought,
surprised by the fierce intensity of her feeling.

She wanted so much for Ted and Lucie to be
happy! She hadn't realised until this moment how
much it mattered to her that her brother and his
bride should have the kind of happy and stable
family life Eve could remember from the days
before her mother had died. Ted had been so much

younger that he didn't really know what he had lost when their mother had died, what had been missing from his life for far too long.

But now, with Lucie, he had the opportunity to create that kind of happiness, and Eve wanted it for him with all her heart. It was what she'd been fighting for all these months and years . . . But it was time to follow the bridesmaids across the terrace and down the steps to the garden.

Eve was made intensely aware of Jack as he relinquished Lucie to Ted and stepped back a pace. Briefly, he was standing next to Eve, and she experienced a fierce wave of longing. She wanted Jack to keep on standing here beside her; she didn't want him to take his place in the first row of seats. She wanted it to be *their* wedding, she realised, feeling dazed. With painful clarity she realised that she wanted the two of them to be standing where Ted and Lucie were. She wanted the minister to be saying the words to *them*; she wanted *them* to be making the responses, so that when the service ended, she would be Jack's wife!

She wanted *everything*, she told herself with passionate intensity—then felt a stirring of guilt as she realised that the service had been proceeding while she had been lost in pointless thought. It was almost over now; she had allowed her brother's wedding service to slip by without paying any attention to it.

This had to stop, she told herself, feeling desperate. She couldn't permit her existence to be so thoroughly dominated by thoughts of Jack Sinclair, and she wouldn't permit herself to be cheated out of the last few moments of the wedding

service because of him. This was, after all, the most
important day in her brother's life, and she forced
herself to put aside her own unhappy longing and
confusion in order to concentrate on the minister's
last few words. For a few minutes she was swept
along on a tide of pleasant sentimentality, savouring
random memories of the years when she and Ted
had been children together and rejoicing in his
current happiness and Lucie's.

It wasn't until the receiving line began that her
own misery returned. From now on, she realised,
the day was going to be a test of endurance. She
knew almost no one among the guests; nearly all
were Lucie's friends, or Ted's, or—most unfortunately—Jack's.

His were easy to identify—slightly older than
the rest, obviously extremely well-to-do, with a
chic sophistication which set them apart from the
others. They were also far too brittle and clever
for Eve's taste. She didn't think they cared in the
least about Lucie or Ted. In fact, Eve suspected
they cared about very little—which made them,
she supposed, perfect friends for someone like
Jack.

During the cocktail hour which followed the
receiving line, Eve observed that the presence of
his friends seemed to encourage Jack to withdraw
even further into himself. It was true he performed
all the duties expected of a host: he circulated and
talked and smiled at all the right times. He even
permitted a stunning frosted blonde to flirt with
him, and appeared to be enjoying her attention.
But his air of detachment appeared greater than
ever; he seemed always to be holding himself apart,

as though unwilling to permit any real contact with anyone.

'Why so glum?' enquired Tony, joining her where she stood alone, an untouched drink in her hand. 'Are you beginning to wish you hadn't been quite so successful in getting your brother married off?'

'No, nothing like that,' Eve answered quickly. Then, seeing Tony's expectant expression, she realised that her honesty had created the need to give him some plausible explanation for her obvious depression. 'It's just that I'm not comfortable. I— I don't feel as though I belong here.'

'I don't suppose you do,' he nodded thought-fully. 'Ted's friends, and Lucie's, all seem terribly young, and we're both getting too old for such robust displays of enthusiasm, aren't we? And Jack's friends . . . well, they're not your sort at all. They're all incredibly calculating, and none of them are real—all the things you hate. I fit in beautifully, of course,' he added with a self-depre-cating smile.

'But you're not at all like that,' protested Eve fiercely. 'You're the *only* person here who doesn't make me feel uncomfortable.'

'But there's Jack, and that jolly little flatmate of yours,' Tony reminded her. 'I can't believe they make you feel uncomfortable.'

'But Jane's too busy circulating—and flirting—to bother with me,' Eve objected, ignoring Tony's mention of Jack. 'Not that I mind, you under-stand,' she added hastily. 'I don't expect anyone to bother with me tonight.'

'I shall,' offered Tony promptly, and Eve wondered if he could possibly imagine just how grateful she was for his offer of support.

With him beside her, she was able to go through the motions of enjoying herself during the elegant dinner and the toasts, and the dancing which followed. She even managed to keep from faltering during her one duty dance with Jack. And that was all it had been, she reflected unhappily when it was over. He had held her at a careful distance, and she had kept her eyes averted, afraid to meet his and see the careful detachment there. She had been stiff and ill at ease, desperately anxious to have the dance end. But when it had, she had felt even lonelier than before.

Still she went through the motions—smiled and laughed and pretended to be having a wonderful time. She even joined in the game of catching Lucie's bouquet, although she felt silly among a pack of twenty-year-old girls. She knew Lucie tried to aim directly at her, but she didn't attempt to catch the bouquet, and one of the girls lunged and came away with the prize.

Later, just before they left, she had a few seconds alone with first Lucie and then Ted. There was only enough time to hug each of them and wish them every happiness before they were on their way to begin their honeymoon. Then, successfully fighting the tears that threatened, she had found Tony again.

The bride and groom might have left, but the party was still in full swing, and Eve threw herself into the festivities as though pretending to enjoy herself would be enough to make it true. Each time she caught a glimpse of Jack, it was a knife twisting within her. He was usually dancing with the same frosted blonde who flirted so charmingly. She had a silvery laugh and a clever way of tilting her head to one side when she smiled up at him, always waiting until she had seen him return it with one of his own.

It wasn't until she and Tony were drawn into a large group of Jack's friends that Eve abruptly discovered she couldn't stand another minute of the business. She'd had enough—more than enough!—and she knew she had to get away. She withdrew from the group, offering some lame excuse about needing to repair her make-up, then fled the party in the striped tent and headed towards the house.

For a while she stood in the concealing shadows on the terrace, but that brought back too many painful memories of the evening when Jack had found her there and she had gone with him to his office—and everything which might have been between them had fallen apart, she acknowledged bleakly, feeling more alone than she ever had in her life.

She had no one. She had never had Jack, and she no longer had Ted. Tony and Jane were friends, of course, but they didn't really count. There didn't seem to be anything left for her, she thought, turning left, away from the brightly floodlit tent and the sounds of the party. Instinctively she started down one of the paths through the garden, pausing only when she reached the vine-covered loggia. She lingered there for a few minutes, until she saw the shadowed figures of a couple enter the garden from the point nearest the tent. Then she fled again, taking the narrower path which led to

the Grecian folly at the edge of the pond. Surely
that was far enough away, she told herself, not
wanting anyone to intrude on her now. She needed
serenity now, a place where she could be truly
alone, and time to sort through all her tangled
emotions.

There were suddenly so many nevers, she
reflected, reaching the gate in the wrought iron
fence that surrounded the folly, fumbling with the
latch until she had the gate open. It seemed that
everything was ending for her—the years of being
responsible for Ted, the years of knowing that the
two of them belonged to each other even though
they were otherwise alone in the world. There had
been such security in knowing those things, she
realised—then checked as she heard a sound behind
her.

But it was only the gate swinging shut. No one
had followed her here, and she went slowly up the
steps to the covered porch, seeking sanctuary
among the shadows there. Far away, across the
broad lawn and then the garden, the house and
the striped tent were ablaze with light, and the
strains of music floated faintly on the air, mingling
with the fragrance of the roses. She leaned against
one of the white pillars, her eyes filling with tears
which dissolved the lights into dazzling, jagged
stars.

Lord, she was a fool to suddenly be feeling so
terribly alone, she told herself as the tears spilled
over and coursed down her cheeks. She had known
this was going to happen; it wasn't as though it
had come as a surprise. This was what she had
been working for these past eight years—to see

Ted through to independence. The only thing she hadn't expected was that it would come quite so soon, or that it would come at a time when she had fallen in love with a man who would never love her in return. She sniffed, wiping futilely at her eyes—then froze as she heard the definite sound of steps behind her.

'Here, you can use this,' Jack told her, emerging from the shadows to hand her a pocket square of white silk.

Obediently she took it from him, wiped her eyes and blew her nose. Why hadn't she seen him? He was too large to be missed, even in the shadowy darkness. He had taken off his jacket and loosened his tie; she could see the narrow black ends of the tie against the brilliant white of his shirt. 'What are you doing here?' she finally found the courage to ask.

'The same thing you are, I suppose—wanting to be away from that,' he explained, gesturing in the general direction of the lights and the music. 'It's a lonely feeling, isn't it?'

'Yes.' Eve stared down at his handkerchief, not quite sure what to make of him now that he was being approachable. 'But——'

'You wouldn't have expected me to be feeling that way,' he finished for her, sounding amused. 'I'm not made of stone, you know, although I suppose you have every reason to think so. But we each lost what little family we had today, and I'm feeling it, too.'

'Are you?' she asked doubtfully, risking a quick glance up at him.

'Yes, although we handle these things differently.

You came out here to cry, while I was merely getting drunk.'

He didn't sound drunk, or anything close to it, and Eve was surprised to think that today had generated enough feeling in him that he had wanted to come out here and get drunk. 'I thought you were still at the party . . . '

'Permitting Louisa to flirt with me,' Jack supplied smoothly, finishing yet another sentence for her. 'No. That began to pall, and I decided that being alone and getting drunk were better alternatives.'

'Then perhaps you'd like me to leave,' she offered quickly, even though she was curiously reluctant to go.

'I'd rather have you stay. Being alone hasn't turned out to be quite as satisfactory as I thought it would be, although getting drunk still seems a good idea. Stay and have some champagne with me.'

'Oh, I don't think——' she began uneasily, but he cut her off yet again.

'I know you don't, but do it anyway! You needn't get drunk with me, but at least stay for a little while. After all, we're both in the same boat tonight, and we might as well enjoy it as much as we can. For the rest of them, it's just a party.' He gestured briefly towards the lights across the garden. 'We're probably the only ones who care about what happened here today.' He left her long enough to go through the doorway into the little room behind the porch, returning a moment later with an open bottle of champagne and a glass. 'Who else really gives a damn?' he asked rhetorically.

'You're not being fair,' she chided, and wondered why she bothered. Hadn't she already thought almost exactly that? 'Surely a few people do!'

'Precious few.' He poured, filling the glass to the brim. 'None of my friends do, and you know that as well as I. Here, you go first,' he directed, handing her the glass. 'We'll have to share, because I only brought one glass. I've got plenty of champagne, though,' he added, staring out across the garden. 'You don't like my friends, do you?' he asked unexpectedly.

'No,' Eve answered honestly after she'd taken a sip of champagne, 'but I wasn't talking about them when I said that a few people must care about Ted and Lucie.' She took another, larger drink of champagne, then handed the glass back to him. 'I was thinking of their friends.'

'And then there's the fellow you've been with.' He drained the glass, then picked up the bottle to pour more. 'I've seen him before, and he's more the type to be one of my friends, yet he seems sincerely interested in you, as well as your brother. The two of you are really quite good friends,' he continued, passing her the glass, 'although not in quite the way you seem to want people to think. You've been flirting outrageously with him, you know.'

'I know.' She drank some more champagne, then gave the glass to him. 'I felt like it,' she said defiantly.

Jack finished the little she'd left in the glass, picked up the bottle to pour again and discovered it was empty. 'Time for another,' he told her, going to get a second bottle, already working at the cork when he came back to her. 'Flirting's not your style,' he continued as the cork popped and he poured again, politely giving her the first sip. 'You've never flirted with me, even when it might have helped your cause. I wonder why you felt like being quite so provocative tonight.'

'You were letting that woman flirt with you,' Eve retorted. 'It's nearly the same thing!'

'And perhaps you're human enough to have been a bit jealous,' he suggested quickly, 'and to have wanted to make me jealous too. If that's true, I don't mind in the least. In fact, I rather like the idea. It suggests that perhaps I matter at least a little to you. It's good to know, tonight, that I matter to someone. I can't expect to matter much to Lucie, now that she's got Ted, and God knows I don't matter to any of them . . . ' He stopped, staring off across the sleeping garden, obviously lost in thought.

Until he reached for the glass she was holding, she thought he had completely forgotten her presence. Then their fingers briefly touched and she knew he hadn't, but he didn't seem disposed to talk. She didn't speak either, but allowed her thoughts to wander while they silently shared the glass. Occasionally, Jack would reach for the bottle to pour more for them, the small sounds of his movements sounding unnaturally loud against the quiet night and the faint music.

It was all quite lovely, she thought dreamily. Standing here beside him seemed to be casting a spell on her. She wasn't sure precisely what sort of spell it was—whether it was something happening between them, the effects of the champagne, or simply that she wasn't feeling lost and lonely any more. Whatever it was, it was making her feel remarkably happy in spite of the fact that she had been very much cut adrift today in the moment when the minister had pronounced Ted and Lucie man and wife.

'We'll have to make this one last,' Jack said unexpectedly, his words punctuated by the popping of another cork. Eve had been only vaguely aware that he had gone back inside the little room to get another bottle, and now she tried to gather her scattered thoughts and focus on his words. 'There aren't any more,' he added by way of explanation as she turned to look at him, 'and I'll be damned if I'll go back there to get more.'

'Why?' she asked, watching while he poured and then handed her the glass.

'Because I don't want to break the spell,' he explained, uncannily echoing what she'd been thinking only a little while before. 'I'd rather be with you.'

'Ah.' She considered that admission while she took a sip. 'Why?' she asked again.

'Because none of them matter to me, and you do.' He took the glass from her, his fingers brushing lightly against hers. 'I don't pretend to understand it,' he continued, a thread of humour in his voice, 'but I find myself thinking about you . . . almost constantly.'

'Oh.' To say that his words surprised her was an understatement of epic proportions, and it also left her feeling vaguely guilty. 'I try not to think about you,' she confessed.

'Of course.' Jack drained the glass, then carefully

poured more. 'That's because you dislike me, and disapprove of damn near everything I do.'

'That's not true,' Eve protested as he handed the glass back to her. Their fingers touched again, and this time she permitted hers to linger against his for a little longer than absolutely necessary. Something was happening, she realised, watching him over the rim of the glass. Her mood, at least, had just shifted. She had been enjoying the easy companionship between them, but now she felt a heady sense of optimism, a kind of unthinking excitement. 'You shouldn't think that,' she whispered, taking a step towards him, her full skirts rustling lightly as they brushed against his legs.

'Eve?' She heard both warning and amusement in his voice. 'What are you doing?'

'Trying to make you see that I *do* like you,' she explained, closing the small distance between them. She lifted her face to his and outlined her lips with the tip of her tongue in the model's trick to make them look moist and inviting. 'I think it might help if I kissed you,' she added, vaguely surprised at this unexpected talent she seemed to have acquired, of suddenly knowing how to tease. 'Do you want me to?'

'You know damn well I do,' he told her, but for a moment she was afraid he was going to resist. She held her breath, waiting, then he caught her by the waist and she knew she had won.

The excitement within her flared, almost suffocating her with its intensity as she parted her lips to meet his. When he would have been gentle, even careful, the depth of her response broke through the last of his reserve and his kiss was suddenly so passionately invasive that she gasped, instantly possessed by a wild and primitive hunger. Her body arched instinctively against his and the glass slipped from her fingers as she locked her arms around his neck. Vaguely she heard the sound as it shattered, but it had no reality for her. Jack was her only reality now, her senses completely absorbed by the contact between them.

'Lord, Eve,' he murmured, his breathing uneven when his lips finally left hers, 'this isn't wise.'

'I don't want to be wise,' she whispered. When he would have tried to put a little distance between them, she slipped her hands beneath the collar of his shirt to trace the firm muscles of his shoulders. 'I want you to make love to me.'

'You didn't the last time this sort of thing happened,' he observed with a little more self-possession.

'This is different.'

'Obviously,' he agreed drily, and she could tell that she was losing. 'This is too much champagne—for which I blame myself—and too much of an emotional day.'

'I don't care,' she insisted, smoothing her hands over his shoulders and on to his chest, then beginning to fumble with the first of his shirt studs. 'It's as good a reason as any,' she added as she heard his sharp intake of breath.

'For God's sake, Eve,' he said roughly, and she could feel his muscles tensing beneath her touch, 'I'm not made of iron!'

'Good.' She worked the first stud free and started on the second.

'You'd better stop,' he told her, but his restraint

was beginning to slip as she removed the second stud. 'This isn't what you want.'

'Yes, it is.' She was getting better at the studs; the third and fourth went quickly, allowing her to push open his shirt so that she could touch her lips to his flesh. Excitement was building within her again, scattering her thoughts and leaving her dizzy with desire. 'It's exactly what I want,' she whispered, absorbing herself in the taste of him and the scent of him and the hard line of his body against hers.

'Then tell me again, when it's not the champagne talking,' he said roughly, taking her by the shoulders and forcing her away from him. 'I think you'd better sleep this off,' he continued after a moment, this time with considerably more self-possession. 'And it wouldn't hurt to remember the things about me you chose not to believe the last time,' he added with an obscure, unreadable smile.

CHAPTER EIGHT

THE ONLY thing that made the next morning bearable for Eve was learning that Jack wasn't there. According to the housekeeper, he had been called away during the night. 'Business, of course,' Mrs Harper had explained, although Eve hadn't believed that for a minute.

She was why he had left, she acknowledged miserably, sitting alone in the dining-room, drinking black coffee while she waited for Jane to emerge from her room. The sounds of the party had continued long after she had escaped to her room, and she was willing to bet that Jane had stayed with it until the very end.

She would probably sleep until noon, Eve concluded, fighting both a splitting headache and a general feeling of wretchedness, pouring herself another cup of coffee in the hope that it might help. Unfortunately, when her head finally did begin to clear, there was nothing to do but contemplate what had happened between her and Jack the previous night.

The enormity of her indiscretion appalled her. She had made an absolute fool of herself—thanks, no doubt, to a combination of champagne, her feelings of being so alone, and the companionship which had suddenly seemed to exist between them. That knowledge wasn't enough to excuse her behaviour; it helped to understand it, but nothing could excuse the wanton and abandoned way she had thrown herself at Jack.

He obviously couldn't excuse it either, which was why he had left during the night. Although he had shown surprising tact and forbearance in preventing her from going even further than she had, he had obviously been anxious not to see her again.

She couldn't blame him for that. She didn't want to see him either, although the fact that she couldn't perversely added to her foul mood!

Fortunately, when Jane finally appeared, she was too full of her own observations of the wedding and reception to subject Eve to a barrage of awkward questions.

'It's rather fun to mingle with the rich, isn't it?' she asked rhetorically, 'and Ted and Lucie's friends were fun too, although very different from Jack's. Whenever I began to feel gauche among the jet-setters, I drifted back to the younger crowd and felt madly sophisticated by comparison. I got propositioned by an undergraduate, a doctoral candidate, a commodities broker and a fellow who doesn't do anything except live off his investments—which is not something that happens every day to me! Pity you went to bed so early,' she told Eve, completely missing the quick wave of colour that washed over Eve's face at her words, 'but I expect you were feeling the letdown of having everything over, and Ted and Lucie gone. And it would have been nice if Jack had stayed too,' she continued, twisting the knife a little deeper. 'He's really absolutely charming when he's in a good mood, and the two of you looked marvellous when you were dancing together. You're both so tall and elegant, and you *fit* together somehow.'

No, Eve objected silently, we don't fit together at all.

Having slept late and lingered over breakfast while she talked, Jane was now in a rush to get back to New York. She was leaving for San Francisco that evening to spend at least a week with a well known sportswear firm, exploring the possibilities of going to work there as a designer.

There were several hours of frantic activity—getting back to New York and to their apartment, getting Jane packed and on her way again. When Eve was finally alone in the apartment, she methodically set about the work there was to do. Until she was ready for bed, activity kept her black thoughts at bay, and it wasn't until she was alone in the dark that unhappiness seized her in its relentless grip. Then, unaccountably, she cried not because she was alone, but because she had ruined any slim chance she might have had with Jack.

She clung to work, activity an antidote to misery as she forced herself to keep busier than she ever had before and tried to make plans for an empty future. She refused to examine the sources of her misery, refused, in fact, to *feel*. That worked best, she found. It made it possible for her to accept the news when Jane called from California to say that things looked promising about the job and that she would be staying at least one more week.

Even more important, it made it possible for her to survive when Ted and Lucie called a few days later.

Their honeymoon had been the beginning of their trip to Alaska, where Ted was going to study a small tribe of Eskimos and the way in which their cultural heritage was in conflict with modern technology. Ted and Lucie called from Fairbanks, on the evening before they started even farther north to the village where they would be living for most of the next year.

'But I'll write,' Lucie had promised solemnly. 'I'll have all the time in the world, so I'll keep you posted on everything. And you must write often too,' she commanded. 'We're going to want to hear all your news, and to know that you're all right. I'll ask Jack to find some time to see you once in a while,' she concluded casually.

He wouldn't, Eve knew, but she couldn't say that, couldn't even permit herself to feel the despair that knowledge caused. Nor could she cry, when she finally hung up the telephone. And when, a few days after that, Jane returned from California, Eve couldn't permit herself to feel a fresh sense of abandonment when she heard Jane's news.

'I've got the job,' Jane announced triumphantly. 'They liked my work, and I've been offered a good contract, and I'm to start as soon as I can get myself moved!'

'That's wonderful,' Eve told her, and meant it. She knew how hopeful Jane had been about this possibility, and how tired she had been of the uncertainty of freelance work. 'You must be so pleased!'

'Well, I am,' Jane agreed, and now, instead of sounding enthusiastic, she seemed sheepish, 'but I wasn't sure you would be. I hate to move out on you like this, with almost no warning.'

'I'll miss you,' Eve said briskly, 'but we always knew this wasn't an arrangement for life! You'd be mad to refuse a job like this!'

'But I'll worry about you,' Jane explained. 'I don't like the idea of you being alone just when you've lost Ted. It seems like too many things happening at once.'

'But I'm not going to be lonely,' Eve told her, deciding this was the time to announce her own plans for the future, crystallised during too many empty evenings. 'To be perfectly honest, I probably wouldn't have been much company for you. I'm going back to college.'

'Now that you don't have to work Ted's way through any more,' Jane supplied drily. 'But that's no great surprise. You've always said you'd do it when you were done paying his bills, but it's going to cost you more to live, without me to contribute half of the rent.'

'Don't worry about that, for heaven's sake,' said Eve calmly, although sounding unconcerned was an effort. She hadn't considered the financial aspects of Jane's move, and paying all of each month's rent was a major and unexpected expense. 'Look, I can get another flatmate,' she continued. 'The agency is forever trying to find apartments for new girls to share, so I won't have any trouble.' It was true, she reflected, but she

very much hoped she'd be able to manage withou
the presence of a stranger in the apartment. Being
alone, she thought grimly, was better than some
of the alternatives!

Eve had always considered herself to be self-
sufficient and independent; she knew she still was
but now she realised just how much she had
relied on Jane's company at the end of each day
Without that easy companionship and casual
conversation, the evenings seemed endless, and
Eve finally decided something had to be done to
fill them.

She had registered for two evening courses—
the first step towards a college degree, but they
wouldn't start until after the first of the year. To
fill the time until then, she found a couple of
evening lecture series to attend—anything to
occupy her time.

Coming home from one of her lectures on a
Wednesday evening in early November, she finally
faced the fact that the defence mechanism which
had been keeping her from feeling anything was
now breaking down. She was always vaguely
unhappy now, she could no longer keep the
loneliness away, and at night she lay awake
contemplating a future which seemed to offer
nothing.

Perhaps, she reflected, she had chosen this
night to finally admit her unhappiness because
she was so much more tired than usual. The day's
heavy work schedule had made it necessary to go
straight from her last booking to the lecture
Now, as she walked the few blocks to her apart

ment, fatigue had settled on her like a thick grey fog, causing her to feel even more depressed than usual.

But fatigue might help her to sleep, she thought as she turned the last corner and started down the block, fixing her eyes on the dim light over the entrance to her building. She had only another fifty feet to go when the figure of a man detached itself from the shadows of her building and moved in front of her.

There was almost no time to react. One moment she had the pavement to herself and in the next she found her way blocked. Later, she would remember an instant of dull confusion before she saw the man reach for her and heard the obscenities he was muttering more to himself than to her. Then she was screaming, striking out at him, doing all the things she'd often mentally rehearsed but had never needed before. A part of her mind stood apart from what was happening, telling her she had to get away, that there would be no one to know what had happened to her, no one to even know that she hadn't come home, if she didn't manage to fight off her attacker.

So she kept on screaming while she kicked at his legs, trying to gouge him with her sharp heels. She struggled when he got his arm around her, and when he pulled her close she went at his face, clawing viciously with her long model's nails. She heard him curse, and there was a brief moment of triumph when he finally released her. Then she felt a blow against the side of her face, driving her back and away until something sharp and very solid came up to meet her head.

The next thing she knew was the sound of voices, someone asking her name, asking her if she had any family. A brother in the wilds of northern Alaska, she thought, and it was almost enough to make her laugh. Instead, she whispered Tony's name, surprised at how much it hurt to do even that. Later, she was aware of the bright chaos of a hospital emergency-room—doctors and nurses and Tony's voice insisting that a plastic surgeon be brought in to stitch her face. There was pain and confusion, and finally one last pinprick that sent her off to sleep.

When she awoke, she had no idea how long she had slept, but Tony's reassuring figure was seated beside her bed. 'Don't try to talk yet,' he advised, smiling down at her when he saw that her eyes were open. 'You've got an incredible bruise on your cheek, and talking will hurt. You've also got three broken ribs, a sprained ankle and ten stitches in your forehead. But you're going to be fine, and the stitches won't show once they heal. Did you understand all that?' he asked, and she nodded obediently, even though that small movement was painful. 'Good. Now I'll get a nurse for you. They only agreed to let me stay because I promised to leave as soon as you woke up. What you need most right now is rest.' He stood up and bent to kiss her undamaged cheek. 'Don't worry,' he said kindly. 'Everything's under control.'

Two days after the attack, the stitches on her forehead looked no better and the bruise on the side of her face was several startling shades of purplish-blue, but the swelling had decreased enough to permit her to talk with a relative degree of comfort. Paradoxically, the rest of her body hurt more than before. Her ribs were exceedingly painful; she couldn't bear weight on her ankle, and fresh bruises had begun to show up on various parts of her anatomy.

Still, she couldn't complain, she reflected as she surveyed her unadorned little hospital room. Everyone had been kind—the nurses and doctors, even the police detective who had come to question her. But it was Tony who had helped the most. He had visited twice since that first night, when he had kept vigil until she had finally come to in the early hours of the next morning. He had just left her now, at the end of evening visiting hours, and she was still sitting up in bed, looking through the stack of newspapers he had left with her.

'You're famous, or at least notorious,' he had teased when he had given them to her. 'The tabloids have had a field day with the attack on your life and virtue!'

She felt notorious, she decided, staring down at the headline: 'Model Attacked—Fights Off Assailant', accompanied by a photograph of her from one of her more exotic fashion shoots.

The story briefly described her injuries, then concentrated on her modelling career. It was obvious that her agency had provided most of the information—in exchange for which, Eve decided cynically, it had been prominently mentioned.

She didn't like the idea of being spread across

the front of a tabloid, but what bothered her most was the fact that the article mentioned that her brother was married to 'the former Lucie Sinclair, sister of multi-millionaire financier Jackson Sinclair'. He'd be furious about that, Eve thought unhappily, imagining what he would think if he discovered himself linked to her under this screaming headline. He'd never forgive her, she told herself—then looked up to find the source of her concern standing in the doorway of her room.

Livid with rage seemed a good way to describe Jack at this moment, Eve decided with a curious sense of detachment. She watched him while he carefully examined the bruise on her cheek and the stitches on her forehead before his gaze finally met hers. Then, when she saw just how cold his eyes were, she nervously laced her fingers together, bracing for his anger.

'You had absolutely no business being out alone at that time of night!' he told her savagely, advancing into the room until he'd reached the side of the bed, putting her at a distinct disadvantage as he towered over her. 'What in God's name were you doing?'

'Not intending to be mugged,' she retorted, instantly on the defensive, 'and it wasn't all that late—only a little after ten. I was coming home from a lecture,' she added, hoping he might think that sounded respectable enough, but he didn't even appear to have heard her.

'You might have been killed!' he began, then broke off, brooding down at her.

Never before had Eve seen him at a loss for

words, and she decided he must be very angry indeed. 'Or raped,' she supplied helpfully, his anger perversely making her bold. 'That would have been better, because they couldn't have published my name in the papers.'

'That's not amusing,' he snapped, going to stand by the window, his back to her. 'You ought to be taking this more seriously!'

'But you're taking the newspaper stories seriously,' she pointed out resentfully. 'That's why you're angry.'

'What on earth are you talking about?' he demanded with what sounded like genuine surprise, turning to face her.

'The one I read mentioned your name.' It was her turn to be surprised—or at least confused. 'It makes such a point of my being a model, and it mentions your name—as though we were really related—and it's all so sordid,' she finished unhappily.

'That's got nothing to do with it, Eve,' said Jack a little more calmly, easing into the chair beside her bed, 'and I'm not angry—at least not with you. I'm angry that it *happened*. I've been concerned since my office reached me and put me in touch with your friend Tony. He said it was morning here, and that this had happened to you the previous night, but it was evening in Singapore, and I'm not entirely sure how many days ago that was. I suppose it depends on whether one is here or there, and the whole thing gets even more relative when you throw in the International Date Line, and crossing it to get back here.'

'You were in Singapore?' Eve demanded with a feeling of disbelief. She hadn't expected Jack to be concerned about *her*, and it certainly wasn't like him to wander, as he just had with his confusing discussion of days and times. 'You surely didn't come all the way from Singapore because of this!'

'I didn't have much choice,' he admitted. 'Tony got in touch with me because he felt Ted should know what had happened, but he had no idea how to get in touch with him. When I finally got through, Ted was worried about you, and he needed to hear more directly what the doctors had to say. I was the obvious one to speak to them, so I came as quickly as I could.'

'But you shouldn't have!'

'You might let me be the judge of that,' he suggested gently. 'None of us was going to be satisfied until we knew how you were—you might try to accept that gracefully, Eve. I've already spoken to your doctor,' he continued casually, 'and he says you can leave here tomorrow, although it will be a while before you can take care of yourself—given broken ribs and a sprained ankle. You're also anaemic, according to the doctor—overwork, I expect. You need fresh air and good food, and someone to fetch and carry for you. That's why I've decided that you're going to Stonegate,' he finished.

'You can't *do* that,' Eve said sharply. 'You can't decide something like that for me!'

'I already have,' he told her, a new note of firmness in his voice. 'You really don't have any alternative.'

'I've got plenty of alternatives,' she snapped, although she couldn't have come up with one at the moment. All she knew was that it was unthinkable that she should be dependent on him or obligated to him. 'I don't need any help!'

'But you do,' Jack said gently, watching her with an unreadable expression. 'God knows you've never let anyone do anything to make life any easier for you, but you've got no choice this time.'

'I won't go!'

'Of course you will. It's the obvious solution, and there's no reason for you to refuse. Unless,' he added thoughtfully, 'you're still remembering the evening of the wedding.'

Oh, God! she thought despairingly, feeling the colour stain her cheeks.

'You shouldn't be, you know,' he said kindly, but amusement still lurked in his voice. 'It's nothing to be ashamed of. I enjoyed myself enormously, and would have enjoyed myself even more if I weren't too much of a gentleman to take advantage of a woman who'd had too much of the champagne I'd been giving her.'

'Please,' she whispered miserably, 'don't make it any worse.'

'I won't,' he agreed promptly, 'so long as you say you'll go to Stonegate. If you continue to refuse, Lucie and Ted will wonder why—and I'm afraid I'll have to explain the whole business to them.'

'That's blackmail!'

'I know,' he agreed with an unrepentant smile, 'but I warn you, you aren't going to win this one.

Cheer up, Eve, it won't be so bad. It's not likely you'll even see me.' He started to get up and then paused, reaching out to take her right hand in his. 'Lord, look at your nails,' he mused, carefully examining them, noting that some were chipped, while the others had broken off at the quick. 'What did you do?' he asked after a moment. 'Scratch his eyes out?'

'I tried to,' she answered awkwardly, wishing he would release her hand, 'but I don't think I did.'

'You must have, from the look of things.' He smiled lightheartedly, suddenly looking years younger. 'Lucky for me that they haven't had time to grow back!' Abruptly, he released her hand and was gone from the room before she could think of a suitable response.

Eve's existence at Stonegate was certainly luxurious, but it was also lonely, in spite of the fact that she was—at least during the day— surrounded by people. Mrs Harper, the house-keeper, supervised a staff which included several maids, a cook, a driver, a handyman, and two gardeners who managed to keep busy even this late in the years as they prepared the grounds for winter. In addition, guards patrolled the grounds at night, with attack dogs to accompany them.

It was all, Eve had to admit, most impressive, but somehow isolating. While everyone was pleasant and co-operative, no one was particu-larly forthcoming, no one encouraged casual conversation, much less any easy friendship.

Like Jack himself, the members of the staff

were reserved and distant—which was probably why they'd been hired, Eve decided. Jack wouldn't want any gestures of friendship, although she wouldn't have minded a few. The only way to relieve her loneliness and occasional boredom was to indulge herself with books from the well stocked library and the vast selection of tapes and records to play on the complicated stereo system in the same room.

During her first full week in residence, the monotony was twice relieved by trips to visit a local doctor. He pronounced himself satisfied with her recovery, nodded approvingly when she told him her ribs didn't hurt quite as much as before and that the rest of her aches and pains were nearly gone. On her second visit, eight days after she had been attacked, he removed the stitches from her forehead and told her she could go for walks, so long as she didn't try to overdo it.

With the stitches gone the scar on her forehead was nothing more than a thin line, and even the bruise on her cheek was beginning to fade. On the whole, she was looking and feeling more human, she reflected on the Saturday evening that marked the end of her first full week at Stonegate.

She had finished her solitary dinner and was now completely alone in the main part of the house, curled up comfortably on the couch, wearing a housecoat and reading a good book. Handel's *Royal Fireworks Music* was playing loudly on the stereo, filling the silence of the house, and there was a fire on the hearth to add

life and cheer to the room. She was feeling
particularly contented, she reflected, getting up
to use the poker to re-adjust one of the logs on
the fire. She was becoming accustomed to her
isolation; she was actually beginning to enjoy this
lazy existence, and she was hardly sore at all. Life
was really quite nice, she decided.

Then, as she started to straighten up, she caught
a brief impression of movement on the far side
of the room. Instantly, she knew there was
someone with her, that the loud music had
covered any warning sounds. She had been
tempting fate to decide that life was quite nice,
and all the guards and attack dogs in the world
couldn't keep out someone who wanted to get in!

She panicked. Until the night she had been
attacked, physical violence had been an abstrac-
tion. Now, instantly, the darkness of that night,
that street, were upon her again; she felt the same
terror, saw the same shadowy figure blocking her
way, heard the same muttered obscenities . . .
Acting on instinct alone, she gripped the poker
more tightly and turned, swinging it wildly.

'Eve!' The sound of her name only barely
penetrated, but she felt the poker encounter
resistance just before it was wrenched from her
grasp. 'Eve,' Jack said again, sounding amazingly
calm, and in the silence that followed she heard
the poker clatter to the floor. 'Poor girl, I didn't
mean to frighten you.'

That much cut through her terror, but what he
said next was so much meaningless gibberish to
her. Simply to focus on him was more than she
could manage. Her mind was working frantically,

trying to comprehend the fact that it *was* Jack—
not a faceless stranger in the street—standing
before her. She was going to faint, she realised,
swaying on her feet. For the first time in her life,
she was going to faint. She felt sick; the world
was growing even darker and steadily receding,
the only reality Jack's grip on her arms.

She gave up then, stopped trying, aware of
nothing until she found herself on the couch.
Jack was beside her with his arm around her
shoulders, supporting her as he forced her head
down to the level of her knees. 'Poor girl,' she
heard him say again, and when she finally drew
a deep and steadying breath, he asked, 'Better
now?'

She nodded, although she wasn't entirely sure.
Her skin was clammy and she was shivering. 'I'm
sorry,' she apologised through chattering teeth as
he permitted her to straighten up. 'I thought——'

'Yes, I know what you thought,' he agreed
grimly, but she could feel the concern behind his
words, and that was her undoing.

'And I was afraid——' She wanted to continue,
but she was suddenly shaking too much to be
able to speak.

'I know,' he said again, gathering her into his
arms, holding her close.

She could feel the warmth of him, the strength
and safety he represented, and she burrowed even
closer, her face pressed against his shirt as she
started to cry.

'That's right,' he murmured, his lips against
her forehead. 'Let it all out.' One arm was still
around her, holding her close while the other

hand smoothed back her hair in a curiously comforting gesture. 'Don't stop until it's all out.'

'I didn't know—I didn't know it was there,' she finally managed when the racking sobs had given way to quieter tears, her face still buried against his chest. 'I hadn't thought about it—it was as though it had happened to someone else, and I'd only heard about it afterwards. I didn't realise how frightened I'd been.'

'I know,' he soothed, 'and I had to blunder in and bring it all back! Still, you've got to face the ghost before you can lay it.'

'I've certainly done that now!' Eve pulled away with an apologetic smile. 'And I've cried all over your shirt.' She reached out to touch the damp spot where her face had pressed against him, then instantly withdrew her hand. Suddenly, her fear and raw emotion had been replaced by a self-conscious awareness of who he was and of what had transpired between them the night of the wedding. He would think she was taking liberties again, she thought uncomfortably. If she wasn't careful, he'd decide she was going to be making advances every time they were together. 'I'm sorry,' she said after a moment, nervously lacing her fingers together and staring down at them. 'I—I shouldn't have taken it out on you.'

'Why not?' he asked kindly, giving no sign that he had noticed her sudden withdrawal. 'I was the cause of it all.'

'But still . . . ' She hesitated, wishing he wouldn't be kind. It only confused her, and tonight was no time for confusion. 'I think I'd better go to bed now,' she finished abruptly.

'All right.' Jack was on his feet instantly, and when she started to rise, he picked her up in his arms, holding her close against him again.

'You shouldn't do this,' she protested weakly, even as she instinctively slipped her arms around his neck to steady herself. 'You really can't.'

'Of course I can—very easily, in fact. You hardly weigh a thing.' There was amusement in his voice, so she knew he was teasing her, but there seemed to be something more—a kind of raw emotion which made her believe that he cared. 'Besides,' he continued as he carried her out of the room and across the hall, then started up the stairs, 'for once in your life you might give in gracefully and let someone take care of you.'

'You're a fine one to say that!' she objected with a grand sense of freedom, deciding there was no reason why she shouldn't rest her head on his shoulder. 'I don't believe you've ever let anyone take care of you.'

'You're right,' he agreed, and even without looking up to see his face, she could tell he was smiling, 'but I don't see what that has to do with anything. Do you know,' he continued when he had reached the top of the stairs, and her mind unconsciously registered the fact that he was still breathing evenly, as though carrying her had been no effort at all, 'I can't remember when I've ever bothered to take care of anyone else—at least not quite in this way.' He pushed open her bedroom door and carried her into the darkened room, setting her down only when he reached the bed. 'I'm enjoying myself,' he explained as he

carefully unbuttoned her robe and slipped it off
then pulled back the sheet and blanket so tha
she could get into bed. 'I don't suppose it wil
last,' he mused lightly, his tall figure silhouettec
against the light from the hallway. 'It's probably
just a passing fancy—a novelty—but it *is* pleasant
I'll revert to type soon enough, I suppose,' h
added more briskly.

But he hadn't yet, and she watched as his dark
form bent towards her. 'Goodnight, Eve,' h
whispered, tucking the blankets around her befor
his lips briefly and very gently touched her cheek

CHAPTER NINE

'DID YOU sleep well?' Jack enquired politely when they met the next morning at breakfast.

'Yes, thank you.' Eve coloured slightly, remembering the previous evening, the way she had fallen apart. 'You were very patient . . . very kind.'

'It was nothing.' He gestured dismissively, and she caught a brief glimpse of a straight, angry line across the palm of his hand.

'Did I do that?' Without thinking, she reached across to turn his hand, examining the seared flesh. 'I did, didn't I?' she asked, still holding his hand when she looked up to meet his gaze. 'With the poker. It was still hot, and you had to take it away from me. I'm so sorry!'

'Forget it,' he told her coolly, withdrawing his hand. 'Forget the whole business.'

As though she could, she mused, sipping her coffee while he finished his breakfast. She hadn't realised the extent to which those brief moments of struggle in the street had been weighing on her. Now that she'd been through the emotional storm—faced the ghost, as Jack had put it—she felt somehow lighter and more like herself again. She couldn't forget what he had done for her, but it was obvious that *he* could. In fact, he already had. He had reverted to type with a vengeance—all cool composure and distance.

'I'm here because Lucie wanted me to come,' he said bluntly when he had finished eating. 'Actually, she put it a little more strongly than that. She was furious to think I'd only seen you once in the hospital, then shipped you off here to be alone—*her* words.'

'I'm hardly alone with so many servants around,' Eve pointed out, determined to match his cool approach, 'and they've all been very kind.'

'But servants don't count, as far as Lucie's concerned, and I realised I'd better come up and see you, if I want to stay in her good graces. I intend to call, later today, to assure her that I've done all that I ought, and to report on your continued progress.' He paused and leaned back in his chair. 'You should call too. It's all very well for me to tell them how you are, but they'd feel better to hear it directly from you. I don't think we should mention last night's little episode,' he advised, eyes narrowing briefly. 'It would only worry them. Wiser, I think, to concentrate on the fact that your stitches are out and that the remarkable bruise is fading. You *are* better, aren't you?'

'Much.'

'Good.' Abruptly, Jack got up. 'I've got to leave now, but I'll be back in another couple of weeks—for Thanksgiving.'

'There's no need,' Eve began awkwardly, but he waved aside her objection.

'There's every need—believe me. I've already taken entirely too much abuse from my sister; I don't intend to take more. I'll see you, Eve.'

Was that a promise or a threat? she wondered, brooding over her coffee after he had left the room. Last night seemed to have further confused an already tangled situation. The problem was that he had been *too* kind, *too* understanding. She had felt so safe and protected in his arms, and now she was tempted to romanticise the incident—and Jack—far more than was wise.

She shouldn't be romanticising him at all. He had certainly made that clear enough in the past, and his reversion to type this morning had provided all the confirmation she needed. She was a fool—a fool in more ways than one, she told herself, listening as the front door closed behind him.

'Here's a promising sign,' observed Jack, announcing his presence from the doorway. 'You didn't attack me with a hot poker this time. Waiting up for me, Eve?'

'Of course not,' she corrected crossly. She had spent the entire day waiting for him to arrive. By evening, when she had been forced to pick halfheartedly at the Thanksgiving feast served to her alone, she had finally given up on him. 'I didn't think you were coming.'

'You should have known better. I always mean what I say.' He advanced into the room, loosening his tie and shedding his jacket, then pouring himself a drink. 'I don't suppose there's any food left,' he said hopefully.

'There's tons of it. Do you want me to fix you some?'

'If you don't mind,' he told her politely, sitting down opposite her, pausing to sip from his glass. 'I don't believe I've eaten today, but I hate to bother anyone at this hour—except you, of course. But that's nothing new, is it?' He smiled briefly at the thought, but his amusement did nothing to disguise the tired lines in his face. 'I seem to spend an inordinate amount of time bothering you.'

As he was now, she thought as she started for the kitchen, although not in the way he usually did. What was bothering her this time was the potential for a comfortable kind of intimacy between them. There was no challenging hard edge about him tonight, and that frightened her. She had done a great deal of thinking during his absence, finally coming to the firm conclusion that she had to make a clean break, but his present mood threatened to weaken her resolve. It would be easy now for her to be lulled into a false sense of security, to forget just how cold a man Jack was, to believe there could be something more between them . . . And she mustn't believe that, she told herself firmly as he appeared in the kitchen doorway, drink in hand.

'You seem to know where everything is,' he observed, watching as she worked.

'I helped clear away after I ate,' she explained, putting some of the leftover gravy on to heat.

'Did you?' he asked with real interest, taking the carving set from her and beginning to work at the nearly untouched turkey. 'That's a compliment, you know. Mrs H doesn't take kindly to strangers in her kitchen. If she let you help, she must have decided to accept you as one of the family.'

'Which I'm not.'

'But you are. You're my brother-in-law's sister,' he pointed out with a teasing smile as she put together a plate of food.

'That doesn't count,' she said sharply, trailing behind him when he took the plate from her and went back to the library. This sort of thing couldn't continue, she decided, watching as he poured himself another drink. She had to stop things now, before they went so far that she got badly hurt!

When he had finally settled on the couch and begun to eat, she perched on the edge of the chair opposite, her hands twisted together in her lap. 'Jack,' she began, taking a deep breath, deciding it would be easier to make a clean break, and to be firm about it, 'I want to go back to New York. Now.'

'What? Tonight?' he asked, glancing up at her with a curious smile. 'Isn't it rather late?'

'Of course not tonight,' she explained impatiently, 'but tomorrow, or whenever it's convenient. I don't have to go back on your plane, but I will need someone to take me to the airport.'

'No,' he said mildly enough, but there was a hint of steel beneath that one syllable. 'There's no need for you to leave.'

'There's no need for me to stay either,' she countered. 'I'm perfectly fit now. My ankle doesn't give me any trouble, my ribs are healed, the bruise is gone from my face, and I can use make-up to hide the scar on my forehead. It's time for me to go back to work.'

'No,' he said again, impatient this time.

'What do you mean—no?' she demanded, torn between confusion and anger at his sudden high-handedness. 'You can't make me stay when I want to leave!'

'I can make sure that there isn't any way for you to leave,' Jack countered grimly. 'You're not ready to go back. You may be better physically, but that's not the only thing to consider. You've been through too much emotionally, and I don't want you alone in the city this soon.'

'*You* don't want me . . . ' Eve trailed off, briefly speechless. 'Haven't *I* got anything to say about it?'

'No,' he answered flatly, pushing aside his plate. 'You've got to learn to take better care of yourself. You were *attacked* , for God's sake!' he continued, clearly irritated, as though in some obscure way he considered the incident to have been her fault. 'You might have been raped or even murdered, and you can't go back until something has been arranged to make sure that it won't happen again.'

'There's no way to make sure it won't happen again,' she retorted, 'and you can't make a decision like that for me.'

'But I have,' he told her, his cool detachment infuriating her.

'God, you're a cold one!'

'That's right,' he agreed evenly. 'It's the habit of a lifetime—bred into me, you might say. First my grandfather, then my father, then me. All of us cold and hard and determined to have our own way—which is why you're not going back to New York until *I* say you can.'

'You have *no right*!' Eve exploded, shaking with anger as she got to her feet, determined for once to be able to look down at him. 'You have no right at all! No one gave you the right to run my life! Damn you,' she snapped, turning away before she lost control to the point of clawing at his impassive and unrevealing face. 'You can't *do* this,' she finished as she stalked from the room, slamming the door behind her for good measure.

Once in her room, she spent a long while pacing from one end to the other, her arms wrapped tightly around her, as though in that way she could contain the rage within her. He had no right, she kept repeating, no right at all to keep her here against her will. He had no right to keep her here in his house, where she was dependent upon him, and where he could see her—torment her—any time he pleased!

She had to get away, before things got any worse, any more complicated for her! She would have to explain herself more clearly—not tell him the truth, of course, but advance reasonable, rational arguments, ones which would appeal to his reasonable, rational mind. There was nothing to do but approach him again—calmly this time—and keep at him until she'd won his agreement.

And no time like the present, she decided impulsively. She knew he was still downstairs; even in the midst of her turmoil, she would have heard if he had come up the stairs and gone to his room. He was probably working in his office by now; late hours didn't mean a thing to him, and it was better to get the issue settled now, before his position became any more inflexible.

Without hesitation, she left her room and started silently down the stairs. When she reached the first turn, she could see that the corridor leading to his office was dark. He'd either gone out for a walk or was still in the library, she guessed, reaching the bottom of the stairs. She wasn't about to search for him in a cold, dark garden—particularly when there were guards and attack dogs to be considered. But the door to the library was still closed, perhaps from when she had stormed out. It seemed likely that Jack was still in there, and she hesitated for only a moment before she opened the door.

'For God's sake, turn that off,' Jack said roughly, and it was only when he spoke that Eve realised she had automatically flipped the light switch on the wall when she had seen that the room was dark.

She had a brief glimpse of his long form stretched out on the couch, then she turned off the light, wavering uncertainly. 'What's wrong?' she asked at last, because it seemed obvious that something was. He hadn't sounded well; he'd sounded as though he wasn't in complete control—and that wasn't like him. 'Are you sick?'

'I've got a splitting headache.'

'Migraine?'

'No,' he answered with brief economy, sounding, she thought, more than a little ragged around the edges.

'Are you sure?' She advanced slowly into the room, guided by the dim glow of the fire. 'It sounds like migraine,' she told him, stopping beside the couch. 'Jane gets them once or twice a year, and she always sounds like that.'

'I don't care what Jane sounds like,' he said irritably. 'This is nothing more than too much work and too little sleep.'

'I see.' She nodded, then couldn't resist throwing back at him the words he had used on her only a short time before. 'You've got to learn to take better care of yourself.'

'Don't be clever!' He shifted slightly, and even in the dim light from the fire, she could see his brief expression of pain. 'You might make yourself useful instead. Would you get my pills? They're upstairs, in the cabinet in my bathroom.'

It was the first time Eve could remember him asking her for anything. The first time she'd ever heard him ask anyone for anything, come to that, she reflected as she left the room without another word. On her way upstairs, she detoured briefly to the kitchen and started coffee, having learned a thing or two about headaches from Jane.

Upstairs, she was halfway across Jack's bedroom when its impact struck her, and she stopped dead to study it more carefully. As in the rest of the house, there were plenty of fine antiques, but there was nothing welcoming or cheerful about this room. Above dark wainscoting, the walls were covered with antique leather of a deep maroon shade, only barely relieved by a faded decoration of gilt painting. The curtains at the windows were a dark red and

gold brocade and matched the hangings and the
cover on the massive four-poster bed. Even the
Oriental carpet was dark—shades of maroon and
green, with only a little gold to provide relief
from all the gloom.

It looked like a museum, Eve decided with
distaste, as though nothing had been changed in
years. She had the terrible feeling that the room
was exactly as it had been in Jack's father's day—
even in his grandfather's day. 'The habit of a
lifetime—bred into me. First my grandfather,
then my father, then me,' he had told her, and
she could feel those three lifetimes bearing down
on her as she stood in the centre of the room.

But this wasn't accomplishing anything, she
scolded herself, going quickly into the bathroom
to find Jack's pills and then heading back
downstairs. In the kitchen, she poured a cup of
strong coffee and added just enough cold water
so that it wouldn't be too hot to drink. When
she finally returned to the library she waited for
Jack to comment on her delay, but he said
nothing as he carefully levered himself into a
sitting position and held out his hand for the pill
container.

She watched as he fumbled two of the pills
into his hand, then passed him the coffee. 'Drink
the rest of it,' she directed when he had washed
down the pills and would have set the cup aside.

'I'm not in the mood for coffee,' he told her,
sounding even more irritated and ragged than
before.

'Coffee helps,' she said firmly. 'Hasn't anyone
ever told you that?'

'No. Why?' he asked briefly.

'It constricts the blood vessels, which are the problem in the first place,' she explained, standing over him until he had drained the cup. Then she took it from him and watched as he leaned back against the couch, closing his eyes. 'If you're going to have bad headaches, someone ought to tell you useful things like that.

'Someone just did,' he pointed out, 'but I don't believe it.'

'You will before long.' She pulled up a footstool and sat down a couple of feet away from him, reflecting that this was the moment when she ought to offer to massage the tense muscles of his back and neck. In all the novels she had ever read where the hero had a headache this bad, the heroine always did offer. The offer was usually accepted too, Eve mused, and then one thing led to another . . . but she wasn't going to fall into that trap!

'It's no wonder you get headaches like this,' she observed after a moment, deliberately choosing to be unsympathetic. 'I got a good look at your bedroom.'

'I fail to see the connection.'

'You would,' she acknowledged drily, 'but it's a terrible room! I bet nothing's been changed but the sheets for three generations—but that's the tradition isn't it? Just like your father and your grandfather, you put so much effort into making money and shutting people out of your life . . . and then you take it out on yourself this way.'

'Is Freudian analysis one of your specialities?' he asked impatiently, but she thought that he sounded just a little better than before.

'No. It's just that you're not quite as unreadable as you like to think you are.'

'Apparently not to you,' he agreed, and she decided he definitely sounded less ragged. 'But then you'd see it more clearly than most, because you aren't so very different yourself.'

'At least I let people into my life!'

'But only on your own terms, Eve,' he pointed out. 'You've got just as much pride, you're just as stubborn, and you're no more willing to let people help you than I am.'

'I let you help me the last time you were here,' she reminded him, 'and you've just let me help you.'

'I didn't have much choice just now,' he explained with the ghost of a smile. 'I let this go too long.'

'Well, you shouldn't, you know,' she said seriously, remembering more of what she had learned from Jane's experiences. 'You only make things worse when you do.' She paused, halted by a quick pang of guilt. 'This started when I was raging at you, didn't it?' she asked unhappily. 'Why didn't you *say* something to stop me?'

'I don't recall being given a chance.' Jack smiled again, cautiously leaning forward to rest his arms on his knees. 'Besides, I wouldn't have anyway—you ought to know that. I may let my headaches get out of control, but never myself. At least I never did before you insinuated yourself into my life.'

In the silence which followed that surprising admission, a log crumbled on the hearth, sending brief flare of light into the room. Before the shadows returned, Eve got a better look at his face and decided it didn't seem quite so drawn and tense.

'It's better, you know,' he said at last, confirming her judgment. 'My headache. Nearly gone, in fact. You were right—the coffee was very effective.' Eve was suddenly aware that his words were beginning to slur. 'I don't seem to be thinking very clearly,' he added after a moment, sounding mildly surprised.

'Then you'd better go to bed,' she said firmly, standing up.

'But you don't approve of my bedroom,' he objected, obviously amused at the thought.

'Well, short of redecorating it tonight, you haven't any choice. Are you all right?' she asked with concern as he got to his feet, swaying alarmingly.

'Not entirely. Perhaps I could lean on you,' he suggested with exaggerated politeness. 'It's not a trick, Eve,' he added after a moment, correctly reading her sceptical expression. 'No dishonourable intentions. No intentions at all.'

She got one arm around his waist while his hand gripped her shoulder, holding her captive against him until they reached the staircase, where he could shift his weight to the handrail. When they reached his room, he released her completely, leaning against the wall while she opened the door and found the light switch again.

'What made you come down, I wonder,' he mused, 'just when I needed you most?'

'I was going to try to discuss things rationally,'

she explained, turning back to him. 'About my
leaving, I——'

'Not now, Eve,' he interrupted to say, straight-
ening up and gripping the edge of the doorframe.
'I won't be able to understand a word you say.'

'Will you be all right?' she asked doubtfully,
studying his face.

'Offering more help?' he asked with an unreadable smile. 'Better if you don't, I think,' he added
after a moment, carefully turning away from her
to enter the room. For a few seconds she watched
him, before she also turned away, hating to see
the way that sombre room seemed to be absorbing
him into itself.

The next morning, Eve was surprised to find Jack
in the dining-room when she came downstairs.
Even more surprising was the fact that while he
looked a little pale, he seemed otherwise no worse
for the previous night.

A maid appeared with fresh coffee, and Eve
took perverse pleasure in asking for a large
breakfast on a morning when Jack obviously
wanted none. 'You weren't in very good shape
last night' she said when the two of them were
alone again.

'To be honest, I don't remember very much—
not after the headache went away. Did I make a
complete ass of myself?'

'No.'

'I must not have made any improper advances
either,' he observed. 'If I had, you'd be watching
me the way a rabbit watches a cobra about to
strike. No, not a rabbit,' he corrected after a

moment's thought. 'More like a mongoose, I think—prepared to fight me to the death, if necessary. God knows, you were angry enough last night——' He was forced to pause when the maid appeared with Eve's breakfast. '—and you were right,' he resumed when she had left. 'I don't have the right to decide your life for you. If you're determined to go back to New York, we'll leave today.'

'Well, that's unexpected.' Eve regarded him with lively curiosity. 'What brought about your sudden change of heart?'

'It's not a change of heart, Eve—surely you know that,' he chided gently. 'I've merely changed my mind—seen the error of my ways, if you like. I spend too much of my time telling people what to do, deciding their lives. Most of them—almost all of them, in fact—put up with it, but you're different . . . ' He broke off to stare at some point beyond her, his expression unreadable. 'Then, we'll leave as soon as you're ready,' he said briskly, almost savagely. 'I hope to God *that* pleases you!'

So she was different, was she? Eve mused as she completed her packing, wondering if she should be feeling this vague sense of optimism. Still, Jack had said she was different, and while he had refused to admit a change of heart, he had come close to apologising to her. That was different too. He was softening just a bit, she concluded happily, snapping the last of her suitcases shut. There was something between them which had never been there before.

But that something was conspicuously absent during their drive to the airport, and her optimism faded fast. Jack was as cold and impersonal as he had been the only other time they had made this trip. With careful politeness, he had asked for her forbearance while he finished some work, then had produced a file and opened it. Watching out of the corner of her eye, Eve decided that the only promising sign was that he didn't appear to be accomplishing much. Only rarely did he turn a page or make any notes, and there were long periods when he merely stared straight ahead apparently deep in thought.

'Why are you so anxious to get back?' he asked, finally breaking the silence between them, putting his papers aside when the plane had taken off. 'You seemed happy enough at Stonegate and you've made it clear that you don't like the work you do. Why the rush to get back?'

'I've got to start making money again,' she explained carefully. 'I couldn't expect you to give me house room for ever, and I hope to have enough saved by the end of the summer to be able to go back to college.'

'At *your* age?'

'I'm not that old,' she snapped. 'Lots of people go back in their twenties or thirties.'

'But why you?'

'So that I won't have to model any longer. I don't have many years left anyway—I'm getting too old for it—but I want to be done with it as soon as possible. I want a degree, so that I can earn a living some other way—*any* other way,' she continued heatedly. 'I've spent eight years feeling like a piece of meat, something to drape clothes on. You can't know what it's like,' she finished abruptly.

'No, I can't,' Jack agreed thoughtfully. 'So what will you study?'

'I don't know.' She shrugged uncomfortably. 'When I was in school before, I was strictly a liberal arts major—dabbling in anything that interested me. I was learning for the sheer fun of it, and I never gave earning a living a thought.'

'You thought some man would marry you and make all that unnecessary,' he suggested.

She nodded. 'I wasn't very liberated, was I? Not very wise, either. I should have been majoring in something practical. Then at least I'd have some work done, and I'd know what I had to finish. Now I've got to figure out what major I can finish the soonest, given the courses I've already taken—*if* I can save enough money,' she finished uneasily, wishing she hadn't reminded herself of that grim reality.

'Is there any doubt?' asked Jack casually. 'After all, you managed to pay for Ted.'

'Yes, but I was working all the time, which isn't the same thing as trying to save it all up in advance,' she explained unhappily, 'and I've gotten terribly behind by missing so much work this month. It's not going to be easy to catch up.' In fact, it might be impossible, she added bleakly to herself.

'Don't look so worried,' he advised kindly. 'You've managed to do everything else you've set your mind to. There's no reason to think you won't pull this off too.'

He was right, she assured herself, but without much conviction, watching as he took up his papers again, absorbing himself in his work.

CHAPTER TEN

EVE unlocked the door to her apartment and stepped inside, forgetting, for the moment, Jack's presence behind her. Inside, the air was stale and musty; the living-room impersonal without its usual minor clutter, a thin layer of dust covering each flat surface. As though she'd been gone for months, she thought, looking slowly around.

Had this ever been home? she wondered, overcome by a sudden wave of longing for what she had left to come back here: for Jack's place, with its warmth and comfort and cheerful, glowing colours. What had she lost . . .? What was she *losing*? she asked herself, then fought to repress that thought. She gained a moment, standing with her back to Jack while she carefully unbuttoned her coat and tossed it on the nearest chair. Only then, with her composure more or less restored, did she finally turn to face him.

'Well,' she began, forcing a bright smile, 'are you satisfied? You've brought me safely home.' They'd argued that point after the plane had landed. He had refused to listen to her objections when he had informed her that he would see her to her apartment. They had argued again when the car had stopped outside the building and Eve had discovered that he intended to come up with her. Now there was nothing left to argue, she realised, keeping her smile firmly in place. There was nothing at all left—except to say goodbye. 'Thank you, Jack,' she began, determined to finish on a politely impersonal note. 'I'm very grateful for all you've done for me.'

He took her hand, his own so large that hers seemed lost in it. 'You're making this sound very final, Eve,' he said after a moment, his expression unreadable as he studied her face. 'Are we going to see each other again?'

'Of course,' she assured him, still determinedly cheerful. 'Any number of times, I expect. After Ted and Lucie get back——'

'That's not what I meant,' he told her, his tone unexpectedly teasing, his fingers suddenly encircling her wrist to draw her closer. 'I'm not talking about family occasions. I'm talking about seeing you because we want to see *each other*.'

'Oh! I don't know.' Eve was suddenly unsure. Did she want to be wise, or did she want Jack? It was hard to know, she thought, staring down at her hand, seeing how he held her. His fingers were resting only lightly on her wrist, but she sensed that the pressure would increase if she tried to pull her hand away. And he was so close . . . it was hard to be logical or rational when he was so close, hard to know what to do or say. 'I'm not sure,' she began again, cursing herself for not knowing what to say, for feeling so self-conscious, for making the moment so awkward. 'I'm going to be awfully busy . . . working so much, saving money for school——'

'Let me do it for you,' he offered with such a devastating smile that she began to think her legs weren't going to support her much longer.

'Do what?' she asked vaguely.

'Pay your expenses, of course.'

That shocked her back to coherence. 'I couldn't let you!'

'I don't see why not,' said Jack carelessly. 'We're family, after all.'

'Not really!'

'I know,' he agreed absently, 'but what does it matter? I want to do this—do something—for you. It would please me.' He paused to study her face, his gaze holding her as effectively as his hand. 'It would be something between us,' he resumed, but she didn't think he was so much talking to her as thinking out loud, 'something a little more real than the fact that your brother married my sister. You intended this to be the end of things between us,' he continued, and now he was speaking directly to her. 'Didn't you?'

'I don't know.'

'I think you did, but I don't want that.'

'I don't either,' she felt compelled to tell him, casting caution to the winds.

'Good.' He smiled his satisfaction, folding her into his arms. 'It's the same for both of us. Isn't it?'

'Yes,' she admitted helplessly, her lips already parting as he bent his head to hers.

'Lord, I don't know what I want,' murmured Jack, his lips teasing lightly at hers as she leaned against him and slipped her arms around his neck, her fingers tangling in his hair when she pulled him closer. 'But this would be so easy,' he breathed just before his mouth closed over hers with a savage hunger that instantly kindled a fire within her.

It was easy, Eve realised, the fire burning more fiercely as his embrace moulded her body into his. She couldn't resist. The wanting was too strong—an endless, spiralling need that threatened to consume them both.

'Eve . . . Eve, I can't get enough of you,' he said unevenly, his hands at her waist, slipping under her sweater to begin to trace intricate patterns on her skin, inflaming her even more. Then she felt herself falling, pulled down until the two of them were lying together on the couch, her body resting on the hard line of his, their lips nearly touching.

'Kiss me, Eve,' he commanded, and now it was her turn to tease at his lips, to feel his tension increasing when his mouth sought to capture hers. 'Perhaps this *is* what I want,' he said thickly, his hands brushing lightly across her breasts until she had no choice but to surrender, to allow his mouth to possess hers.

'It's not the champagne this time,' he observed with lazy satisfaction when their kiss finally ended. 'It it?'

'No,' she admitted, beyond any thought of resistance as he worked quickly to remove her sweater, shifting until the weight of his body could close over hers. It was all sensation now, his lips and his hands against her skin as she fumbled with the buttons of his shirt and heard his sharp indrawn breath when she finally got them free.

'Oh, this is so good,' he murmured raggedly,

his lips tracing the curve of her breast, creating new and unimagined ways to excite her, ' . . . so good . . . but it can't possibly last . . . '

His words barely registered, but she sensed his sudden stillness and knew he was fighting for control. 'No,' she whispered, pushing aside his shirt so that her hands could explore further, prepared to do anything to make this magic last. 'We don't need to stop.'

'But we do.' She felt him ease slightly away from her, creating a little space between them. 'We'll only make things harder if we keep this up.'

'But why?' she demanded, staring up at him, seeing the rigid set of his features as he forced himself to withdraw.

'Because we don't want the same things,' Jack explained harshly, increasing the distance between them. 'I want pleasure and you want sharing, and I can't give you that. I can't give you any of the things you want and have every right to expect.'

'But you have!'

'You're wrong,' he snapped. 'You know I won't love you!' The words hung in the air, making her feel cold and sick. 'It's the family tradition—three generations. Remember? Eve, you want love,' he said firmly. 'You have every right to expect it, but it's the one thing I won't give—don't know *how* to give—and you'd always feel I was withholding a part of myself. If we don't stop this now, the time will come when you'll hate me.'

He broke off long enough to find his cigarettes

and light one, while she automatically pulled on her sweater. 'You know I'm right,' he resumed after a moment, glancing briefly in her direction. You knew it would come to this. Didn't you?' he demanded, turning to face her.

'I was afraid it might,' she said evenly, 'but I think I was wrong. The problem is,' she continued with a rueful smile, 'that you won't agree if I tell you what I think. You'll use your same old arguments, and then I won't agree, and we'll go round in circles for the rest of the day.'

'No point to that, is there?' asked Jack with an answering smile.

'No point at all,' she agreed gently, watching as he got up from the couch and started for the door. 'But I do think you're wrong,' she told him as he opened the door. 'You're having a little trouble admitting it to yourself, but I think you do know how to love. Given enough time to work it through, I believe you'll be able to do it.'

Eve did nothing to stop him from leaving. After all, there was no point in prolonging the argument. For the time being he needed to be left alone, needed time to think things through in a logical fashion, needed time to discover that logic wouldn't work. He needed time to realise that there was nothing logical about the way they cared for each other and permitted themselves to be cared for, each by the other. That was love, and Jack was mad to think that he couldn't love her! He already did, and when he found that logic wouldn't work, he would finally believe what she had told him.

He finally called on Sunday evening, when Eve was already preparing for the next morning's visit to her agency. 'This is Jack,' he began, unnecessarily identifying himself. 'I think we'd better talk. I'd come there, but I've got a crisis on my hands. I've got to be in Rome first thing in the morning, and there's no time . . . Will you come here instead?'

'Come where?'

'To my office. I've sent a car. It should be there in fifteen minutes.'

He was taking a lot for granted, she reflected when she heard him break the connection, but she wouldn't—*couldn't*—hold that against him. After all, he'd done what she'd hoped he would do. In just a short while, everything would be settled between them.

She rushed to be ready in time, choosing a conservative wool skirt and sweater, twisting her hair up in its usual knot, bothering with neither make-up nor jewellery. *This* visit to Jack's office would be different in more ways than one, she thought as she paused long enough to inspect herself in the mirror. There was nothing of the trendy, sophisticated model about her appearance tonight, nothing to displease him . . .

Not that she needed to worry about displeasing him this time, she reminded herself, checking the street from the window, seeing the long black Mercedes already double-parked below. Tonight's meeting was going to go according to plan, just as she had imagined it. Perhaps Jack would even ask her to go to Rome with him, she decided optimistically, slipping into her well-tailored wool coat and starting down to the car.

The executive headquarters of Sinclair Enterprises were surprisingly busy for a Sunday evening, she noted as she followed the same young man through the spacious corridors. Offices which had been dark and empty the first time were now alive with lights and the sound of voices, people either working at their desks or moving from one room to another. A crisis, Jack had said, and from the look of things, Eve decided it must be a major one. It was a wonder that he'd found time for her; the fact that he had was simply another sign that his change of heart was complete!

Then, when she entered his office, she felt the first stirrings of unease. He was seated at the enormous teakwood desk, so absorbed in the papers before him that he was completely unaware of her presence. She was trying to summon the courage to announce herself when he finally glanced up.

'There you are. Someone should have told me.' His brief smile gave her no clue to his feelings. Standing, he indicated the chair on the other side of the desk, then seated himself when she did. 'It was good of you to come at such short notice,' he began again. 'I've given considerable thought to what's happened between us, and I think I've found a solution to the problem.'

'What do you suggest?' Eve asked carefully, still not sure what direction he was planning to take.

'We could agree not to see each other,' he explained. 'That's one way to handle things, but it doesn't please me. It's no real solution—just a way to avoid the issue. I don't see the point, and it's going to be difficult to accomplish when Lucie and Ted come back. Besides, there are too many logical reasons to settle things differently. I think we should marry,' he finished abruptly.

There was no doubt now about the direction he'd chosen to take—not when he talked about 'logical reasons'! 'I can't help but wonder why.'

'Because it makes perfect sense,' he answered, the situation becoming easier for him just as it became more difficult for her. 'There are no reasons *not* to marry, and plenty of reasons why we should.

'We're compatible,' he continued, warming to the subject—in the same way he might warm to the subject of a merger, Eve thought. 'We've spent enough time together to establish that. We find each other sufficiently interesting, so there shouldn't be any danger that we'll get bored. There's plenty of physical attraction between us, and it's obvious that you've become more comfortable with that aspect of things, so that shouldn't be any problem for you.' He stopped.

'Is that all?'

'No.' Jack shook his head before he looked up to meet her gaze. 'If that *were* all—compatibility and physical attraction—I wouldn't see any need to be married. But there are considerable inducements for each of us, I think—sufficiently good reasons to make marriage an attractive proposition.

'I should like to have a family after all,' he explained, his voice completely devoid of emotion, 'a son to carry on the name and the business. I would expect that much of you, although it needn't be accomplished immediately. For you, the advantages are less tangible, but equally real. If you marry me, you won't have any worries.'

'Perhaps you could be more specific,' she suggested, amazed to find that her voice sounded as empty as his.

'Isn't it obvious?' he asked with mild surprise. 'You won't need to worry about saving enough to go back to college, or about earning enough when you're done. You rejected my offer to pay your expenses, but that issue doesn't exist once we're married. You can go back to college without having to be practical, without having to come up with the quickest way of earning a living. You can learn for the sheer fun of it,' he pointed out, and Eve suspected he was deliberately using the same words she had when she had explained things to him. 'But the most telling argument seems to be that you'll be done with modelling. You admit you hate it, and you can stop immediately.

'You've got everything to gain, Eve, and nothing to lose,' he summarised dispassionately, 'unless, of course, you continue to insist on my complete capitulation.'

'I never insisted on that, Jack,' she corrected. 'All I've ever asked is that you love me in return.'

'Yes . . . well, the two of us have very different views of that particular concept, and there's no point in thinking we'll ever agree. I don't love you, Eve; you'll have to accept that. But I can promise you'll never have to worry that

I've fallen in love with someone else.'

He smiled briefly, a cold and meaningless expression. 'I'm prepared to make more of a commitment to you than I would to anyone else. I'd do my best not to shut you out of my life, as my father and my grandfather shut out their wives. Even if I tried that,' he added with a slightly more human smile, 'I don't believe you'd permit it. You'd nag me and hound me as unmercifully as you have since the moment we met. You'd force me to behave myself!'

'And you wouldn't resent that?'

'Of course not!' He seemed genuinely surprised that she would even raise the question. 'I'd expect it, in fact. I don't see that we'd have much of a marriage if you didn't.'

'I don't see that we'd have much of a marriage anyway,' she retorted. 'We can't, in the circumstances.'

'Of course we can!' For the first time, a little impatience was beginning to show. 'We'd have all those things I've already mentioned—companionship, compatibility, physical attraction, children in time. I don't see why we should be prevented from enjoying all that, simply because you're so determined to hear me say I love you. I won't lie, Eve, and I'm simply not willing to love anyone.'

'What you've just described sounds very much like love to me,' she countered.

'But it's not,' Jack corrected with a fleeting expression of distaste. 'Love is something very different; it's irrational and unpredictable and far too uncontrollable for my taste.'

'That's rubbish!' snapped Eve, suddenly goaded beyond endurance. 'You're a fine one for words, but they don't mean a thing! You've got to be the most unpredictable person I've ever met, and I can think of a few times when you haven't exactly been in control of yourself. That's irrational, if you ask me!'

'Which I didn't,' he cut in coldly.

'Of course not, because you knew you wouldn't like what I'd say! What's wrong with you?' she demanded recklessly, past caring what she said. 'All the things you say you don't like about love are the things you don't like about *yourself*! You go on about three generations of cold men, and bad marriages running in the family, but that's just an excuse—something to hide behind. You're afraid to be yourself—God knows why—and you're prepared to do anything to avoid it!'

'Damn you,' muttered Jack savagely, 'don't try that kind of Freudian analysis on me!'

'Why not?' she countered with vicious abandon. 'It's true, and I'll try anything I please on you!' They were both shouting now, she noted, briefly distracted, both on their feet, glaring at each other across the vast surface of the teakwood desk. 'Damn *you*, Jack,' she resumed, gathering the scattered fragments of her bitter thoughts. 'You're doing your best to ruin everything between us, but I'm not supposed to tell you what I think. If you seriously think we can have a marriage—much less one we'd enjoy—in those circumstances, then you're a fool!'

'And you'll be a bigger one, if you turn me ~vn,' he retorted unpleasantly. 'There's too much in it for you, and nothing but a bleak future if you don't accept my proposal.'

'Then I'll take the bleak future. It's better than the empty shell—the business deal—you're trying to offer me.' She stopped abruptly, turning away and heading for the door.

'Damn it, Eve, I'm not through with you yet!'

'Well, I'm through with you!' She paused, her hand on the knob, to deliver a parting shot. 'Perhaps you've forgotten—you've got more than one business crisis to settle tonight. Consider me the failure, and see if you can't do better with the other one.'

'Don't tell me how to run my business! We're going to settle this now.' Jack moved so quickly that he was just behind her, following her through the outer office. 'You might give some thought to how you can expect to support yourself in the future,' he pointed out, so furious that he didn't appear to notice there were other people in the room, all trying not to stare. 'You'd be mad to refuse!'

'I already have,' snapped Eve, making for the corridor leading to the elevators. 'I can't be bought, and you're the one who's mad—to think that I'd even consider such a plan!'

'You'd damn well better!' He was still shouting, completely oblivious to the fact that people were coming to stand in open office doorways, following their progress with frank curiosity. 'I won't permit you to refuse,' he continued, hard on her heels when the elevator doors slid open and she got in. 'Damn it, Eve, I *want* you!'

'Well, you can't have me! Even rich men don't

always get what they want, Jack,' she told him,
her voice shaking with fury as she spaced each
word for emphasis, 'and you won't get me—ever!
You could have had me, if you'd been prepared
to admit that you love me, and you'd have had
my love in return. But you get nothing—nothing
at all!—if this business arrangement is all you can
offer.'

'It's the best offer you're likely to get!' The
elevator had reached the lobby, and now Jack's
hand was gripping her arm, forcing her to keep
pace with him until he could bundle her into the
waiting Mercedes. 'Ah, Eve, be reasonable,' he
told her, getting in beside her as soon as he had
told the chauffeur to take them to her apartment.
'Don't refuse me because of a silly whim.'

'Is it a whim to want you to love me?' she
demanded bitterly, retreating to the far end of
the seat. 'Is it silly to refuse to marry you if you
won't say you do?'

'Of course it is.' Without warning, he moved
towards her, catching her by the shoulders and
trapping her in the corner of the seat, leaning
close. 'We've got something far more reliable
than love. We like each other—at least we do
when we're not fighting like this . . . and we
want each other,' he continued, his voice dropping
to a husky murmur as he drew her into his arms.
'You know damn well we do.'

'No! I *don't* want you,' she raged, refusing to
respond, forcing her body to remain rigid against
his. 'Not now! Not when——'

She got no further as his mouth closed over
hers. At first he was just an angry as she. While

she struggled to free herself, he kissed her with invasive, punishing intensity. But he knew her too well, she acknowledged reluctantly when his tactics changed. He knew how to please her, how to win her submission, and now his mouth was merely teasing at hers as her struggles ceased and she finally began to respond.

'That's right,' he breathed, ending their kiss when, without conscious thought, her arms went around his neck and she began to move restlessly against him. 'Now you kiss me, Eve.'

She had no choice, she admitted with both helplessness and despair. This hungry desire between them wasn't love, but it was no less real. Obediently she lifted her lips to his, her fingers tangling in his thick, crisp hair. She couldn't help herself, and her body, her will, surrendered as she sought an even greater closeness between them.

'You see?' he asked some unknown time later, his words and the note of triumph in his voice cutting through her scattered thoughts. 'You want me just as much as I want you.'

'You're not fair,' Eve complained weakly, her head resting on his shoulder, 'and this isn't love.'

'True, but it's enough,' he said confidently. 'You'll see that, when you've had a little time to think things through.'

'There's nothing to think through.' She sighed wearily, the motivating force of her anger completely destroyed. 'You know how I feel.'

'You'll change your mind,' he assured her with supreme and calculating confidence. 'We'll discuss this whole business when I get back.'

'I won't,' she protested without much conviction.

'Of course you will,' murmured Jack, his lips against her cheek, his hand brushing lightly beneath the hem of her skirt to rest warm against her thigh. 'But if you won't,' he continued as her control began to slip away again, 'I'll find another way to convince you. This one should work very well.'

'No . . . '

'Yes! Don't fight me, Eve.' His lips captured hers with savage force, and now his control over her was so complete that she wanted even that. 'Four days,' he said, his breathing as uneven as hers. 'Four days . . . five at the most. I'll be back by then,' he promised, but it sounded more like a threat or a warning, 'and we'll settle everything between us.'

But she wouldn't be there, Eve told herself as the car stopped in front of her apartment building. There was no way to fight him; running away was her only choice.

CHAPTER ELEVEN

EVE knew that before she saw Jack again she was going to have to harden her heart and focus her anger, find a way to defend herself against his persuasive presence. She needed time—more time than the four or five days he was prepared to give her—time to regain her composure, time to gather up the tattered remnants of her resolve.

Her first impulse was to call Jane in San Francisco and ask if she could bunk in with her old flatmate for a while. But there was no use in even thinking of that, she realised. She couldn't afford the price of the air fare; for the same reason she ruled out a retreat to a hotel here in the city. Instead, first thing the next morning, she called Tony.

'Eve dear, I'm working,' he chided gently when he finally came on the line, 'and it's not like you to bother me during the day. Besides, I thought you were still at Jack Sinclair's place, recovering from your wounds.'

'No, they're gone now,' she explained vaguely, then got to the point of her call. 'I need a place to stay for a while, Tony, and I wondered if I could stay with you.'

'Stay with *me*?' echoed Tony, genuinely startled before he regained his air of cool sophistication. 'Why should you want to stay with me? Haven't you got a perfectly good apartment of your own?'

'Yes, but I've got to be somewhere else for at least a few days—perhaps a week or so. Could I come and stay with you? Starting Wednesday, perhaps?'

'That presents a few complications, you know. Having you underfoot would cramp my style, dear, so you'd better have some very good reasons for needing to stay here—none of which I have time for now,' he added hastily. 'Come and see me this evening, why don't you? You can explain yourself then.'

'You look like hell, dear,' Tony observed when he had admitted her to his deserted studio and provided her with a cup of strong black coffee. 'Your stitches have healed nicely, but it doesn't look like you're getting much sleep. You'd better start at the beginning and tell me what's wrong.'

Obediently Eve did so, finding release and comfort in finally pouring out the whole story. She omitted only a few of the most intimate details, reflecting that Tony was worldly enough to fill in those blanks for himself.

'So what's the problem?' he asked, perplexed, when she was done. 'You're in love with him; you know he's in love with you, and he's asked you to marry him. I don't see how it could be any more simple! What is it? Have you decided to run away just because he won't say he loves you? Just because he won't say the words?' he demanded, sounding impatient. 'Some of us don't, you know. We aren't good at saying those things, but we show women how we feel—and it's pretty

obvious that Jack has done that. You're holding
out just because he won't admit how he feels?'

'Of course,' Eve answered indignantly. 'Don't
you see? It's what you told me when I'd first met
him—that I shouldn't settle for what he was
prepared to give, that I shouldn't settle for
crumbs!'

'I'd hardly call marriage a crumb,' Tony
pointed out. 'I'd say it was a major concession—
the ultimate one, in fact—from a man like Jack
Sinclair.'

'But it's not enough! I refuse to marry him on
his terms!'

'Personally, I think you ought to marry him
on any terms he cares to offer. However, if that's
how you feel, just say no.'

'But he won't let me do that,' Eve tried to
explain. 'He's so good at controlling everyone
around him, and he'll control me, if I give him
the chance. He plans to come back from Rome
in a few days and make me give in.'

'How?' asked Tony, not missing the revealing
colour that flooded her face.

'By——Damn it, Tony, you're a man! You
should know how men can get women to do
things.'

'Are you talking about what might be called
sexual persuasion, Eve?'

'Yes,' she admitted miserably, her voice a thin
whisper.

'But, Eve dear, that's what love's all about,' he
explained gently. 'Jack loves you—wants you—
so much that he's prepared to do whatever it
takes to make you agree to marry him. And you

love him—want him—so much that you can't
resist. That's love! Nothing could be clearer.'

'It's not clear, and it's not love,' she snapped.
'It's just Jack—wanting his own way and doing
anything he can to see that he gets it. He's not
being fair!'

'And you are, I suppose, by trying to run
away?' Tony asked with an ironic smile. 'Sorry,
dear, but it won't wash—at least not with me.
You'll have to find some other bolthole, or else
go back to your own place and face the music. If
you want my advice, which I'm sure you don't,
that's what you'll do.'

'I don't have much choice,' Eve observed
bitterly, only barely able to control the impulse
to throw what remained of her coffee in his face.
'You were my only hope—the only person I
could turn to right now—and you've just let me
down.'

'Perhaps,' Tony agreed, watching unmoved as
she stalked to the door. 'But once you've seen
Jack, you may just find that I was right after all.'

Men! Eve fumed that night as she tried to go to
sleep. They were all alike, and they all stuck
together. They were a cruel and heartless lot—
none more so than Jack and Tony—and she
didn't stand a chance against either of them.
Tony had refused to help her, and in a few days
Jack would be back to force her into a cold-
blooded business proposition of a marriage.

There didn't seem to be any way out, certainly
none that she could see. Jack was too strong for
her, too strong and too sure of himself and his

ability to control her. The worst of it was that he had every reason to feel that way. He would do whatever it took to make her agree, and it wouldn't take much. He would pull her into his arms and start kissing her . . . and that would be more than enough. A little more of that and she'd be a helpless, hopeless case, prepared to spend the rest of her life accepting whatever crumbs he chose to give her. It didn't bear thinking about, but she did for a very long time, until sleep finally overtook her.

At first, in the darkness, she confused the sharp sound of the door buzzer with that of the alarm clock. It wasn't until she'd found the button on the clock that she realised her mistake. Then she was instantly wide awake. The luminous dial on the clock told her it was nearly five in the morning, no time for anyone to come to her apartment.

Still, it was with a detached and almost unthinking fatalism that she got out of bed. She went down the hall and into the living-room, not bothering to switch on a light until she was there. For a moment she stood motionless, staring at the door while the buzzer continued its staccato tattoo. Then she shook herself out of her frozen immobility to lean close to the door. 'Who is it?' she called, although she knew the question was unnecessary.

'Jack.'

'You aren't supposed to be back yet,' she said coldly when she had the door open. Then, when she really saw him, something happened to her. Her universe seemed to shift slightly, and she found herself caught hopelessly off balance. He was leaning against the outer edge of the doorjamb, looking worn, clothes crumpled, and he'd never been as dear to her as he was at this moment. 'Oh, Jack,' she whispered, fighting the impulse to throw herself into his arms.

'May I come in?'

She nodded, stepping back from the open door. She had no choice, no choice at all, she realised, feeling dazed. Jack wasn't going to have to force her to accept his proposal, wasn't going to have to be clever or use his particular powers of persuasion. She was going to do whatever he wanted—gladly and without reservation. This *was* love, she knew, rocked by the sudden insight. Even if he never called it that, never admitted it to her or himself, it was love that kept drawing them to each other. Tony had been right after all, and his words must have been working on her since the moment she'd heard them.

But could she really be sure? she asked herself, hesitating on the brink of belief. It was all so unexpected . . . still so new! 'Would you like coffee?' she asked, buying time.

'If it's not too much trouble.'

'Not at all.' She retreated to the kitchen, grateful for the opportunity to put some distance between them. 'It's only instant,' she told him, clinging to the commonplace when she saw he had followed her. 'I hope you don't mind.'

'Of course I mind,' observed Jack with grim irony, and she couldn't tell if he intended amusement or irritation. 'I don't even like the idea of instant coffee. I don't believe I've ever had it before, which makes it marvellously appropriate now. Do you realise just how many unpalatable ideas I've had to accept since I met you?'

'No.' She concentrated carefully on the task of filling the whistling kettle and putting it on the stove, afraid to look at him.

'Too many,' he said sourly. 'That's what you do best, and you've made an absolute shambles of my life. I didn't have any problems until you barged in,' he continued while she stood with her back to him, staring fixedly down at the kettle. 'I liked my life! I didn't see any need to change it, and I've fought you every step of the way.'

'I know.'

'You don't know the half of it,' he snapped. 'You've been driving me mad since the moment I first laid eyes on you. At first I thought it was simply physical attraction—hardly surprising, given the fact that you're not hard to look at and the additional fact that I'd never before permitted myself to feel anything but physical attraction for a woman. It should have been very simple. We'd have had an affair, and that would have been the end of it—but I couldn't make it turn out that way. You wouldn't let it turn out that way.

'The first problem was that you weren't like any other woman I'd known,' he continued, sounding almost reproachful, 'and you didn't behave like any other woman I'd known. I knew that the first evening we were alone together, when you made absolutely no effort to attract me—quite the reverse, in fact. When I tried to test you by making a couple of leading comments, you seemed acutely uncomfortable when damn

near any other woman would have leapt at the
chance to capitalise on the situation. And then,
when I kissed you that night, you responded, but
I had the feeling you were surprised and just a
little shocked that you had. The only time you
ever did initiate anything between us, it was really
the champagne at work—not you.

'I didn't know what to make of it,' he said
almost savagely. 'I didn't know what to make of
you. You had spirit and pride and courage, and
you   were   so   innocent,   and   so   damned
attractive . . . and I wanted you in a way I'd
never wanted any other woman. I wanted to
forget all about being careful, about keeping
emotions out of it and avoiding attachments. I
suppose you'd say I wanted to lose control; you'd
be right, and that scared the hell out of me,' he
finished abruptly.

That was an admission, Eve told herself even
as a detached part of her mind realised she hadn't
lit the burner under the kettle. Automatically she
did so, listening carefully as Jack began to speak
again.

'From the beginning, none of this has made
any sense! I couldn't get enough of you, even
though I knew you wanted more of me that I
thought I was capable of giving. All the time, we
kept getting closer and closer . . . I knew how
much I wanted you, but it wasn't until Tony
called to tell me you'd been attacked that I
realised just how much you meant to me.

'By the time I came for Thanksgiving, I knew
I had to have you. I was beginning to think I
couldn't survive without you,' he continued reluc-

antly, 'but I wasn't going to admit that, even to myself. I tried to make you stay at Stonegate and then I tried to get you to let me pay for your education, and when those ideas didn't work, I came up with that grand and glorious business arrangement of a marriage proposal—and was fool enough to think you'd accept me.'

'And furious with me when I wouldn't.'

'Not for long, Eve,' he admitted ruefully. 'I left you, started for Rome, and came to my senses somewhere over the ocean . . . and went through merry hell, trying to get out of my appointments there . . . so that I could get back to you. Do you suppose we could sit down?' he asked in an abrupt shift.

She nodded, finally turning to face him. 'In the living-room, I suppose. There's no place here.'

'I'd noticed,' Jack agreed drily, following close behind as she left the tiny kitchen.

By unspoken consent, they sat down together on the edge of the couch, and Eve was struck by the absurdity of the picture they must make—the two of them sitting side by side, she in her flannel nightgown and he in his crumpled three-piece suit. What she had unconsciously been hoping might be a grand and romantic reconciliation seemed to be taking on all the characteristics of a comic opera. At least she thought that until he took her by the shoulders and turned her towards him. Then, when she saw his expression, the moment was as grand and romantic as any she could have imagined.

'Thank God you didn't accept me,' he mused with an abstracted smile. 'I'd never have come to

my senses if you had. I'd have felt so sure of
myself . . . so *right*! Instead, once I was done
being angry, I regretted so much . . . and
missed you. I didn't know it was possible to miss
someone so much, that it could be so painful. I
wasn't rational—which is what you'd been trying
to tell me all along. Once I accepted that, it all
fell into place.'

'Jack?' she asked, almost afraid now to believe.
'Are you trying to say you've had a change of
heart?'

'Not a change,' he corrected, increasing the
pressure of his hands on her shoulders until he
overbalanced her and she fell back into the
cushions piled at the end of the couch. 'It's more
than that,' he continued, bending over her until
he was so close his breath stirred her hair. 'I
don't believe I *had* a heart—until you came along.'

'But you did,' she objected fiercely. 'Otherwise
I couldn't have fallen in love with you.'

'If you say so,' he conceded absently, his lips
brushing lightly across her forehead and on to
her cheek. 'I'm not going to argue the point.
How can I, when I *need* you so? Need you in
every possible way,' he added, smiling down at
her. 'Can you believe that now?'

She nodded, not wanting to speak, not wanting
to do anything to disturb the magic of this
moment between them. This was a happy ending,
she told herself, her spirits soaring briefly, until
she felt him move away from her. 'What are you
doing now?' she demanded, feeling cheated.

'Going to shut that damned thing off,' he
explained as he got up, and only then did she

hear the shrill whistle of the kettle. 'It may not be bothering you, but it's raising hell with my powers of concentration—and I intend to concentrate on you,' he finished as he disappeared into the kitchen. A moment later the kettle abruptly ceased its racket, and then he was back to stand beside the couch. 'Are we going to be married, Eve?' he asked so casually that she was taken by surprise.

'I—that is—if that's what you want,' she finally managed to say, and saw him smile.

'You know damn well it is,' he told her, stripping off his jacket and then his waistcoat, dropping them carelessly on the floor. 'On your terms, of course, and for the right reasons,' he added as he ridded himself of his tie and then lowered himself down beside her. 'I hope you don't want a big wedding,' he began again, pulling her into his arms. 'Not like the production your brother and my sister went through.'

'But it was a lovely wedding,' Eve reminded him with a teasing smile. 'Wouldn't you like to be married in your grandmother's garden?'

'No. It wouldn't be warm enough now,' he murmured, his lips flickering lightly on hers, 'and I'm not prepared to wait until spring. I'm not prepared to wait a moment longer than absolutely necessary,' he finished absently, sensing the stirring of desire within her.

'But what if I want to wait until spring?' she whispered, slipping her arms around him, pulling him closer. 'We met in the spring, and I think I fell in love with you that first night, when I watched you walk alone in the garden. The moon was rising, and——'

'—it was all very romantic, I'm sure,' he finished
for her, 'but have pity on me, Eve. You disgraced
me in front of my staff; I can't concentrate on
my work, and they all think I'm quite mad.
They're right too,' he continued, increasing the
contact between them, moulding her body into
the hard line of his. 'I'm mad about you . . .
mad to have you. I can't do without you,' he
finished raggedly.

'No?'

'Not any longer——' And the time for words
had passed.

At first his mouth merely toyed with hers, but
it wasn't long before his control and her own
began to slip. Passion flared between them, and
suddenly they were kissing with a wild and primitive hunger which Eve instantly recognised as
something new. It had never been like this before
Jack had never been so free and unrestrained
and she had never responded with such a depth
of feeling. In the past, every other time, she
realised with a sense of wonder, there had alway
been an element of reserve between them. Now
all that was gone, and in its place was something
new and infinitely precious. They could forget
themselves completely, absorb themselves in each
other with such need and desire that it left them
both shaken, without any defences in place.

'You were absolutely right,' Jack said unevenly
some vague and unknown time later, his hand
gently smoothing back her hair. 'There's no
reason, no logic to this. Lord, Eve! I *am* well and
truly out of control . . . and it's so much easier

an I thought it would be.'

'What is?'

'This,' he answered simply, pulling her even
oser. 'To have you with me, to feel the way I
 right now.'

'Then call it love,' she prompted fiercely,
cking her arms around him.

'If it pleases you,' he agreed with an indulgent
nile. 'I love you, Eve. I always will. You *are* my
ve,' he added with a sudden fierceness of his
vn, his lips again seeking hers as the last of the
rriers between them disappeared.

Harlequin Superromance

Here are the longer, more involving stories you have been waiting for . . . Superromance.

Modern, believable novels of love, full of the complex joys and heartaches of real people.

Intriguing conflicts based on today's constantly changing life-styles.

Four new titles every month.
Available wherever paperbacks are sold.

Coming Next Month

2977   RANSOMED HEART   Ann Charlton
Hal Stevens, hired by her wealthy father to protect Stacey,
wastes no time in letting her know he considers her a spoiled
brat and her life-style useless. But Stacey learns that even
heiresses can't have everything they want....

2978   SONG OF LOVE   Rachel Elliott
Claire Silver hadn't known Roddy Mackenzie very long—yet
staying in his Scottish castle was just long enough to fall in love
with him. Then suddenly Roddy is treating her as if he thinks
she's using him. Has he had a change of heart?

2979   THE WILD SIDE   Diana Hamilton
Hannah should have been on holiday in Morocco. Instead, she
finds herself kidnapped to a snowbound cottage in Norfolk
by a total stranger. And yet Waldo Ross seems to know all
about Hannah.

2980   WITHOUT RAINBOWS   Virginia Hart
Penny intends to persuade her father, Lon, to give up his
dangerous obsession with treasure hunting. She *doesn't* intend
to fall in love with Steffan Korda again—especially since he's
financing Lon's next expedition in the Greek islands.

2981   ALIEN MOONLIGHT   Kate Kingston
Petra welcomes the temporary job as nanny to three children in
France as an escape from her ex-fiancé's attentions. She hasn't
counted on Adam Herrald, the children's uncle. Sparks fly
whenever they meet. But why does he dislike her?

2982   WHEN THE LOVING STOPPED   Jessica Steele
It is entirely Whitney's fault that businessman Sloan
Illingworth's engagement has ended disastrously. It seems only
fair that she should make amends. Expecting her to take his
fiancée's place in his life, however, seems going a bit too far!

Available in May wherever paperback books are sold, or
through Harlequin Reader Service:

In the U.S.	In Canada
901 Fuhrmann Blvd.	P.O. Box 603
P.O. Box 1397	Fort Erie, Ontario
Buffalo, N.Y. 14240-1397	L2A 5X3

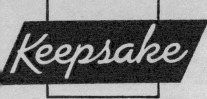

Keepsake

 Harlequin Books

You're never too young to enjoy romance. Harlequin for you . . . and Keepsake, young-adult romances destined to win hearts, for your daughter.

Pick one up today and start your daughter on her journey into the wonderful world of romance.

Two new titles to choose from each month.